Christmas Chateau

De-ann Black

Published 2017

Christmas Cake Chateau

ISBN: 9781521302255

Also by De-ann Black (Romance, Action/Thrillers & Children's books). See her Amazon Author page or website for further details about her books, screenplays, illustrations, art and fabric designs.
www.De-annBlack.com

Romance:

The Sewing Shop
Heather Park
The Tea Shop by the Sea
The Bookshop by the Seaside
The Sewing Bee
The Quilting Bee
Snow Bells Wedding
Snow Bells Christmas
Summer Sewing Bee
The Chocolatier's Cottage
Christmas Cake Chateau
The Beemaster's Cottage
The Sewing Bee By The Sea
The Flower Hunter's Cottage

The Christmas Knitting Bee
The Sewing Bee & Afternoon Tea
The Vintage Sewing & Knitting Bee
Shed In The City
The Bakery By The Seaside
Champagne Chic Lemonade Money
The Christmas Chocolatier
The Christmas Tea Shop & Bakery
The Vintage Tea Dress Shop In Summer
Oops! I'm The Paparazzi
The Bitch-Proof Suit

Action/Thrillers:

Love Him Forever.
Someone Worse.
Electric Shadows.

The Strife Of Riley.
Shadows Of Murder.

Children's books:

Faeriefied.
Secondhand Spooks.
Poison-Wynd.

Wormhole Wynd.
Science Fashion.
School For Aliens.

Colouring books:

Summer Garden. Spring Garden. Autumn Garden. Sea Dream.
Festive Christmas. Christmas Garden. Flower Bee. Wild Garden.
Faerie Garden Spring. Flower Hunter. Stargazer Space. Bee Garden.

Embroidery books:

Floral Nature Embroidery Designs
Scottish Garden Embroidery Designs

Contents

CHAPTER ONE

The Chateau

Lucy's car was filled with her art supplies and two suitcases for the festive trip of a lifetime — to enjoy Christmas and New Year in a traditional Scottish holiday cottage on the estate of a magnificent hotel known as the Christmas Cake Chateau.

Her editor recommended it.

'The chateau is a gorgeous hotel situated in the heart of the Scottish countryside. You'll fall in love with it,' she'd said with such enthusiasm that Lucy immediately pictured it amid the idyllic setting. 'It's got some bland name, the family name of the man who owns it, but because of the architecture and white stone grandeur everyone calls it the Christmas Cake Chateau. Holiday cottages are dotted around the estate. No one will bother you there, Lucy. You'll be free to relax in the cottage and finish those illustrations for the colouring book deadline. No pressures. Get away from the city. Unwind. Finish drawing those new designs. Come back refreshed and ready for the editorial meetings at the end of January.'

Her editor should've written the sales brochure for the hotel. She'd certainly sold Lucy on the idea.

Although she'd set out early that morning from Edinburgh, four wrong detours, lots of stop–offs for tea, and wintry weather caused the day to swiftly become evening and then late night. At almost midnight, the chateau and cottages were all aglow in the snow covered landscape.

The road narrowed, but Lucy kept going, following the directions. She saw the tips of the chateau far in the distance and continued driving in that direction. The whitework of the architecture did indeed make it look like a Christmas cake — one of those traditional cakes with royal icing.

The chateau glistened in the moonlight which was the only light, apart from her car headlamps, illuminating the country road.

Hedgerows, stripped of their former greenery, were sprinkled with snow, reminding her of days when she enjoyed baking and got a bit heavy–handed with the icing sugar for the Victoria sponges.

1

The hedges helped keep her on the road. When the snow obscured the route, she drove between their borders and the car somehow kept going until she finally reached the cottage she'd hired.

It looked exactly as described in the brochure and on the website. The stone built cottage stood alone amid the beautiful scenery. For some reason, the other holiday cottages were situated on the far side of the chateau. At the last moment she'd been upgraded to the cottage on its own.

The cottage was three shades darker than the blue–white snow, and the edges of the roof were encrusted with ice crystals.

A pretty garden surrounded her hideaway and she imagined how lovely the flowers, lawn and border hedge would look in the spring and summertime. In winter, it felt quite magical. A little evergreen grew beside the front door and was adorned with sparkling fairy lights.

Lucy parked the car beside the cottage and stepped outside. Her boots crunched into the deep snow and created the only footprints she could see. It had stopped snowing but the air had a brisk scent promising more snow was on the way. A few stray flakes fluttered on to her dark blonde hair.

She wore a warm jumper over a thermal top and leggings tucked into her boots. Her hooded jacket was cast on the back seat of the car and she was unwilling to put it on. She wanted to feel the wonderful atmosphere wrap itself around her.

In the stillness she held her breath, listening to the silence. Not a sound, not one peep from anything, not even a branch cracking under the weight of the snow or a hardy night creature, whatever they had up here — a winter fox or deer scurrying across the landscape. Nothing. She'd never known anything so quiet. Such contrast to the city with its constant background of people talking even in the depth of night, the drone of traffic, intrusive music, the noises of a city that never knew the meaning of hush.

Lucy looked around. Yes, this was perfect.

She'd been informed in the last email from the chateau booking office that the key to the cottage was under a squirrel. Thankfully it was an ornamental squirrel sitting beside the front doorstep. She was a city girl. Who knew what unusual customs they had in the Highlands. A well–trained squirrel wasn't too far fetched. Was it?

2

The only real contact she'd had with animals was her late aunt's dog with its penchant for snoozing on the floor beside the hall door and doubling as a draught excluder.

Lucy lifted the squirrel and found the key hidden up its crevice.

She opened the door and stepped inside.

The cottage was clean, bright and cosy, decorated in neutral tones and pastels, with pretty vintage and floral prints on the sofa and chair coverings, curtains and bed linen. It had one bedroom, a lounge, kitchen and bathroom. Glass doors from the lounge opened out on to a patio with views across the countryside. From the lounge window she could see the chateau.

In the evening light the white outline of the chateau stood out against the dark sky.

She lugged her bags and cases inside, dumped them down in the hallway, and then went back out to lock the car and take a few minutes to breathe in the splendour of the scenery.

The night sky stretched for miles, and all around were hills and rolling countryside. And the three–storey high chateau. It was magnificent. Her editor had stayed there the previous year but wished she'd booked into one of the cottages for more privacy.

The air was clear and crisp. It was so quiet she felt her heart rate mellow for the first time in months. The hectic pace of illustrating, creating new designs, editorial meetings, more meetings, more artwork and the constant interruptions of flat sharing, that made drawing anything some days a real task, had wound her up so tight.

She shared a flat with one of her dearest friends. Ella had split up with her boyfriend, and the house Lucy and Ella were living in had the lease taken over by someone who wanted to live there rather than rent it out. So they'd decided to share the cost of a flat in Edinburgh. Unfortunately, being an artist, Lucy needed her own space a lot of the time. Time to draw without distractions, without music and people like Ella's new boyfriend popping in and out and bringing their friends back for drinks now and then.

Ella's life was normal. Lucy was the one who didn't have time for anything other than work. She'd illustrated two successful colouring books for adults and now she had to pull another one out of the bag pretty quick. The publishers wanted it for their summer releases. She'd agreed to the deal, banked the advance and set about drawing like mad. The previous books had taken her almost a year each to illustrate and complete the whole design process. This book had to be squeezed into a fraction of that schedule.

And so, with the deadline looming and so much of the book needing illustrated, she'd been advised to leave Ella in the flat. Ella was delighted because she could spend Christmas and New Year with her new boyfriend without having to tip–toe around Lucy's work schedule. Everyone was happy.

All Lucy had to do now was relax — and work.

She could do that — in the cosy little cottage, with no distractions, calm and quietude, time to think, to design, to dwell on fresh ideas. Yes, this really was perfect.

Lucy breathed in the evening air and then went inside to get a good night's sleep.

A fist pounded on the front door of the cottage the next morning.

Lucy assumed it was a member of the hotel staff welcoming her, offering a breakfast menu and generally saying hello.

She opened the door and blinked against the dazzling white snow that outlined a broad pair of shoulders tapering down to a lean, long–legged build.

The most handsome man she'd seen in a while stabbed a finger at his watch. 'Look at the time,' he snapped at her.

'What?'

He leaned down. Stunning blue eyes stared at her. She wished she had lashes like his, long and dark, and in no need of a coat of mascara like hers did.

'Hurry up, Lucy, they'll be here in ten minutes.'

Hearing her name and the urgency in his voice she felt the need to rush and yet she'd no idea what he was talking about.

She did that thing where you look like you're going to go right when you go left instead, and then correct yourself and end up back where you were.

He stepped inside the cottage. His well–cut, dark, silky hair almost touched the door lintel. He wore an expensive winter jacket, black cords and boots. He glared at her comfy leggings and fleecy yarn top with bobbles on it. She'd knitted it herself. Not one of her better designs, but cosy and ideal for a morning in a snowbound cottage. She hadn't been expecting visitors at this early hour of the morning, especially one as handsome and sexy as him. Her stomach

4

tightened and her heart beat quickened looking at him standing there making the cottage feel suddenly smaller.

'You're not even dressed.' The accusation in his tone threw her.

'I *am* dressed. These are leggings and a top.'

'They look like jim–jams.'

She smirked. She said jim–jams, Ella said jim–jams, but this man?

'Don't stand there smirking. Get a move on,' he insisted. 'We're going to be late.'

'Late for what?'

'Please, pleeease get ready. I need you to come with me to the chateau.' His beautiful blue eyes gazed down at her, and her heart gave an involuntary flip. 'Hurry up, Lucy. I'll explain everything on the way there.'

She ran into the bedroom and scrambled through the clothes in her suitcase looking for something warm, appropriate for not being late, and non jim–jammy. The cute Santa top and leggings with snowmen on them (a pressie from her editor) were cast aside.

She jumped into a pair of black trousers and a black top with faux white cuffs and collar. Her boots were brown, her hooded jacket navy blue, but colour coordinating her outfit wasn't an option. She threw her favourite striped scarf around her neck to jazz things up a bit.

Her cheeks were flushed from harassment and in no need of blusher, but she gave her lashes a flick of mascara to emphasis her pale grey eyes, added a touch of lipstick, grabbed her bag and ran through to the hall. He was still standing there. Actually, he was pacing like a wild beast who couldn't wait to get going.

Disapproving eyes glared at her. 'And run a brush through your hair. You look like you've been wrestling monkeys in your sleep.'

That did it.

She thumped her bag down on the floor. 'I'm not going anywhere until you tell me who you are and what you want.'

Her protest vied against something outside that caught his attention. 'That's them. They're here. They're driving up to the chateau. We'll have to run to beat them.'

'Run?'

He thrust her bag back into her hands, scooped her up by the elbows and deposited her outside.

The chateau glistened in the pale, winter sunlight. It wasn't far to run there, but she certainly wasn't making a bolt for it through all that snow. Everything was covered in it.

Before she could object, he grabbed her, threw her with ease over his shoulder and ran like blazes towards the chateau.

Despite yelling at him to put her down, there was something horribly exciting about the situation that she was sure would dwell in her memory forever. The morning a tall, handsome man ran with her across the snow to a magnificent chateau after insulting her clothes and her hair.

From her unusual vantage point it appeared he'd taken a short cut across the chateau's front garden.

She stopped yelling and clung on to the back of his jacket, trying desperately not to accidentally grab his bum.

'Nearly there, Lucy,' he said, seconds before depositing her in the middle of reception. Even from an upside down angle she could see guests glance and smile in amusement. No one seemed in the least bit perturbed. Was this a regular occurrence?

He placed her down gently and checked to see if she was okay before removing her scarf and jacket and ushering her through to a private part of the reception. An office area. His office.

'Excuse me, Struan,' a woman wearing a staff badge said to him, 'they're here. They've parked in the driveway. Should someone go and welcome them?' The woman, in her fifties, looked efficient in her skirt, blouse and cardigan.

He threw his jacket off, revealing a classy Aran knit jumper, and ran a hand through his thick dark hair, pushing it back from his forehead. A few sexy strands tumbled down, refusing to give him the smooth look he was after.

Lucy's stomach did that knotted thing again, and she fought to suppress the attraction she felt for...well, she assumed he was the man who owned the chateau. When studying the chateau's website she'd been far more interested in the cottages, facilities and other things. She'd assumed the owner would be a middle–aged, country gentleman or businessman, instead of a man who wouldn't look out of place as the lead in an action adventure movie. He had star potential. Either that or she was simply in need of some carbs. The delicious aroma of hotel breakfasts being cooked wafted through to the office. Embarrassingly, her tummy rumbled.

'We'll feed you later, Lucy,' he said, and then told the woman, 'I'll be right out, Brona. Give us one minute.'

Brona nodded and hurried away.

He took a deep breath and looked right at Lucy. 'There's no time to explain everything. I'm sure you've done this a hundred times, so I'll sort of follow your lead.'

'Follow my lead?'

'Yes, that's what I'm paying you for. I'm not experienced at dealing with film people. I don't know how to handle them, but we need the publicity, so go out there and do your stuff.'

'I think there must be some mistake. I'm not here to deal with film people.'

He glanced at the computer on his desk. He pointed at the screen. 'Your name is Lucy and you're booked into snowdrop cottage.'

'Yes. I'm here on a working holiday to illustrate a colouring book for adults. My editor recommended it. I've a deadline and we thought this would be the ideal place to draw without any distractions or interruptions.'

He cursed and then said, 'But can you write?'

'Yes, I used to be a magazine journalist.'

'Brilliant. All you have to do is lie and tell them you're my publicity manager and that you'll write a press release for them after they've had a tour of the chateau.'

'What? I'm not—'

'I'll pay you. You can stay in the cottage for free. Just do this. Please, Lucy. I was relying on you...her.'

In the moment she took to ponder her situation, they were interrupted.

'Did you get the message about the publicity girl?' a male member of staff popped his head into the office to ask. 'She cancelled and we put Lucy in the private cottage. She said something about her boyfriend proposing and whisking her off to Bali to get married.' He shrugged. 'I guess you can't compete with that.'

'No indeed,' Struan reluctantly agreed.

Struan gave Lucy a desperate look. 'Please will you do this?'

'Write a press release?'

'Yes.'

Lucy hesitated then said, 'Okay. I can do that.'

7

'And charm them. They're staying for a long weekend to shoot a couple of scenes for a film. Pretend you're my publicity manager. What harm will it do?'

She gave her hair a cursory brush. 'Plenty if I mess things up.'

The words were still in the air as Struan whisked her out of the office to meet them. By now the film director and his assistant were walking up to the front entrance. The director was in his late thirties, tall, slim, casually dressed and quite handsome with a flurry of unruly brown hair. His assistant was a statuesque brunette, chic, attractive, early thirties. She snapped exterior shots of the chateau as they approached.

The director introduced himself to Struan.

'I'm Bret, and this is my assistant Marcia.'

Struan shook hands with them. 'Delighted to meet you.' He ushered Lucy forward. 'This is Lucy. She's handling my publicity.'

Bret smiled warmly. Marcia barely acknowledged her.

'Right, shall we have breakfast? You must be starved. What time did you set off to get here?' Struan said, escorting everyone inside to the breakfast room with its bay windows giving an expansive view of the landscape. The countryside stretched for miles.

'We flew up last night and then drove from the airport hotel this morning,' said Bret. 'Our shooting schedule is extremely tight. My film crew are flying up from London and should be here soon.'

'Their rooms are booked and ready,' Struan confirmed. 'As are your rooms and the exclusive suite for your stars.'

Bret gave them details about his plans for the chateau as breakfast was served by attentive staff.

'As you know, the second unit director is currently filming scenes for the movie at the studios in Georgia, while our location scout found this idyllic setting for the romantic snowscape scenes.'

Lucy sipped her tea, ate hot buttered toast with lashings of marmalade, and let the scenario swirl around her.

'Bret is first unit director,' said Marcia, 'but he's renowned for his hands–on approach to all aspects of his movies, especially when it comes to atmospheric locations.'

Bret seemed used to Marcia's compliments and continued to explain. 'The chateau is perfect for the final scenes. And having a professional help us with the publicity is so important, as is the timing.' He looked directly at Lucy. 'The press don't know we're here and we aim to keep it that way until we've finished filming. Obviously guests may leak the news via social media, but it's not the same as us officially telling the press we're filming here. We want to avoid being hounded by the paparazzi. By the time you've issued the press release, we'll be gone.'

'I won't have to write the press release in a hurry?' said Lucy.

'We need it by this evening,' said Bret. 'I'll email it to my people in Los Angeles who are handing the movie's publicity. They'll okay it, attach the movie's logline and details, add suitable pictures and email it back. Then you'll hold on to it until we're ready.'

'If your people are dealing with the film's publicity, wouldn't it be easier for them to write the press release rather than me?' Lucy asked.

'No, we want a local slant on it, written by someone who is familiar with the chateau, who is able to capture the feel of it,' Bret explained. 'If the Scottish media pick up the story, it'll then end up in the UK national press, and from there the news will circulate worldwide.'

'Basically all I have to do is write about the chateau and the location?' said Lucy.

'Yes,' said Bret. 'We'll add the movie's storyline. We need the Scottish media to understand the nuances of the movie, the underlying motives and the reason why our leading man runs off to the chateau.'

'It's for the love of the leading lady,' said Marcia.

Bret sighed. 'But it's so easy for an action movie to be dismissed as less dramatic, especially when it's a lavish romance with exciting and daring stunts.'

Struan spoke up. 'Stunts? No one mentioned about stunts? Are they being filmed in Georgia?'

Bret shook his head. 'No. Didn't you get my email? Having seen the potential for the movie's leading man, Sanderson Sanders, to come hurtling down the balustrades in the chateau's staircase in the foyer, we're filming them here.'

'Sanderson insists on doing eighty–six per cent of his own stunts. It's written into his contract,' said Marcia. 'We'll take care of all aspects of insurance and safety.'

Bret nodded enthusiastically at Marcia. 'The end fight scenes on the horse–drawn sleigh–ride will look magnificent with the chateau as background. And I may add some impromptu scenes.'

Marcia looked at Struan. 'You said there were stables nearby offering sleigh–rides to guests of the chateau and that we could include them in some of the scenes.'

Lucy saw the whites of Struan's eyes expand as the magnitude of his previous promises were being taken up. 'Yes, I've spoken to them and they're keen to participate. I didn't know about the stunts though. I'd have to tell them about that.'

Bret sipped his coffee. 'Sanderson is an experienced horseman. He won't do anything overly dangerous while galloping across the snow to rescue Charmaine Charlatain and fight her devious ex–boyfriend on the steps of the chateau.'

'It should make for a memorable end scene,' Marcia added.

'Utterly dramatic,' said Lucy, giving Struan a wry glance.

'And there will be an airbag to catch him when he descends from the top of the chateau in the final shot,' Bret assured them.

'This all sounds incredibly. . . exciting.' Struan sounded worried. 'I thought the film was more of a cosy, Christmas romance. You know, one of those warm–hearted films all the family can enjoy.'

'It is,' said Bret, 'except it's action–packed, and with stars like Sanderson and Charmaine, well. . . we're talking awards. . .worldwide distribution. Our vision for the movie has extended.'

'Will you still need the cute Labrador puppy?' said Struan.

'No,' Bret told him. 'We've upgraded the dog to a huge wolfhound.'

Struan sounded as if he was about to panic.' Huge wolfhound?'

Bret laughed. 'Don't worry. We're filming the dog scenes in Georgia. The dog wrangler is US–based.'

Struan let out a relieved breath. 'Thank goodness for that.'

Bret took a bite of his pancakes. 'These are delicious. You'll have to tell me what your secret ingredient is. The flavour is wonderful.'

Donnan, a waiter, overheard and was quick to reply. 'A lavish dose of whisky. Would you like a wee dram to sip?'

Bret nodded. Donnan hurried off and whisked back with several small glasses of whisky and put them down on the table.

'Whisky for breakfast, eh Struan?' Bret grinned across at him.

'I don't usually indulge, but this morning I think I'll make an exception.'

Bret picked up a glass. 'I propose a toast — to exciting times and romance far from home.' He gave Lucy a warm smile.

She hadn't planned on having a drink, but joined in.

Struan downed his whisky and put the glass on the table.

Bret did the same. 'Strong stuff.'

Lucy took a sip and coughed.

'Not used to the hard stuff?' Marcia chided her, swallowing her drink smoothly.

'No,' said Lucy. 'I'm more your ginger beer and lemonade type of party girl.'

Bret eyed her. 'Party girl? We're having a party tonight. Aren't we Struan?'

'Yes, I hope you'll join us, Lucy.'

Lucy squirmed in her chair. 'No, I've a lot of work to catch up on. Busy schedule.'

'You'll join us for an hour this evening surely?' Bret cajoled. 'Are you staying near here?'

'I'm in one of the cottages.'

'Then you really have no excuse for not coming to our party this evening. Persuade her, Struan. Tell her she must come.'

'You must attend the party, Lucy.'

'I have a deadline. My editor is expecting—'

'You work for the press?' Bret said hopefully.

'Not quite. I work in the eh. . . publishing media. And I freelance for clients like Struan.'

Bret accepted her explanation. 'How long have you worked with Struan?'

Struan cut–in. 'Oh Lucy's worked with me for ages . . .'

Lucy smiled tightly at Struan. 'Yet it seems like no time at all.'

'Marcia and I are like that, aren't we?'

Marcia smiled. 'The moment we met, Bret and I clicked. We're on the same wavelength. We get each other.'

'And in this industry, that's a bonus.' Bret tucked into his pancakes and the conversation veered back to the film work.

11

CHAPTER TWO

A Cottage in the Snow

Lucy made her escape after breakfast, and had promised Bret she'd write a press release and email it to him. She'd also promised him a dance that evening — at the party, which she'd become inveigled into attending.

She'd almost reached the cottage when Struan caught up with her.

'Lucy wait, you can't just disappear now. They're expecting a full tour of the chateau.'

'It's your hotel. You don't need me.'

'I do. You're my back–up in case they suss out I'm—'

'Lying to them?'

'I'm not doing it deliberately.'

She froze him with a look.

'Okay, so I am, but I'm cornered. I wouldn't have needed to lie if you'd been the right Lucy.' His expression brightened. 'But Bret seems to like you.'

'That makes things even more uncomfortable. I don't like telling fibs, especially to someone who has invited me to his party.' She shivered as if it made her feel grimy. 'It's all so. . . distasteful.'

'I'm sorry, Lucy. I really am. But surely you see my predicament.'

She sighed reluctantly. 'I do.'

'I'm not the devious type. In fact, I have a reputation for being brutally honest.'

'Such as insulting my clothes, my hair and my supposed tardiness.'

'Yes,' he agreed immediately, then reconsidered. 'No, what I mean is.' He gave up. 'Okay, what would you suggest I do?'

'Let me get on with my work, because I wasn't lying about having a deadline. I came here to work without interruptions and I've endured the complete opposite. Now I'm expected to go to a party tonight. Most people wouldn't call that a problem, but every hour I'm not drawing or planning designs, I'm getting nearer to my

12

deadline and in danger of missing it. This is my career you're messing with.'

He held up his hands. 'You're right. I apologise profusely, but I can make it up to you.'

'You can't make up for lost time. You can't turn the clock back. Time is what I need.'

'Yes, but I could replace some of your time with more relaxing elements where you'd be able to unwind and ponder wonderful designs.'

'Such as?'

'The luxury whirlpool in the chateau. It's all yours at midnight every night while you're here. No interruptions. No other guests allowed. All yours.'

The interested expression on her face gave him hope that she was open to his suggestion.

'It's soothing and very therapeutic, so I'm told. It's available for guests up until 10:30 p.m.'

'Have you ever tried it?'

'I haven't had the time since it was installed in the summer, though I've been meaning to, and probably will after the Christmas and New Year pandemonium.'

'Exclusive use?'

'You can relax in the bubbles to your heart's content and think up whatever it is you do.'

'I illustrate colouring books.'

'Yes, that's what I meant.'

'You really don't get it, do you?'

'I eh. . . sort of. You illustrate stuff.'

'I draw pen and ink floral illustrations. These are printed into books that adults can colour in as a craft hobby, for fun, to relax, to be creative and enjoy.'

'The illustrations are flower designs?'

'Yes, that's been the theme of the past two books. The first was vintage floral designs, the second book focussed on botanical art, and this one is a combination of the two. I've drawn about half of the book — various flowers — bluebells, primroses, tulips.'

'Snowdrops?'

13

'No, I haven't designed them yet, but they're on my to–do list. Snowdrops, crocus, Christmas roses, holly, along with birds, bees, butterflies and foliage.'

'Sounds wonderful. I'd buy it.'

'If I don't put in the hours, the designs won't be ready. The publishers have paid me an advance and my editor is relying on me to do this.'

'I understand, and I'd love to see some of your illustrations when you're not too busy. Maybe I could pop round later with afternoon tea and more apologies in exchange for a peek at your new designs?'

He smiled and she noticed how attractive he was without the constant frown he'd worn since she'd met him.

'Afternoon tea would be lovely. It'll make up for lost time if I don't have to stop to cook and prepare tea.'

'You'll be fed, watered and pampered today. Unobtrusively.'

She smiled and hurried into the cottage.

'Thank you again, Lucy,' he called to her. 'You're a star.'

The press release was relatively easy. She'd written numerous releases and features in her past life working in magazine journalism. Bret had detailed what he wanted the media to focus on, which made it even easier to highlight the main aspects of the film, the choice of location due to its sheer beauty and magnificent architecture that matched the director's vision of what he pictured for the end scenes. Details of the chateau were gleaned from the hotel's website. She had more than enough information to create an interesting release. No doubt Bret's people would tweak it, but she'd written plenty for them to work with.

She'd set up her laptop, scanner/printer, artist light box and other items on the dining table in the lounge. The set–up suited her perfectly. Plenty of room to sketch, and then illustrate each page on to layout paper ready for popping in the scanner.

She'd just finished the press release and emailed it to Bret, when there was a knock on the door. Struan, she thought. She'd recognise that insistent knock anywhere.

Wearing her fleecy yarn bobble top, comfy leggings and a pair of knitted socks, she padded through to the hallway to let him in. Her hair was tied back in a ponytail and she smoothed the stray wisps from her face before opening the door.

'Afternoon tea, as promised.' He stood on the doorstep holding a picnic hamper containing scones, cakes and delicate sandwiches.

He stepped inside and went through to the kitchen where he proceeded to set up afternoon tea for two. He'd also provided a small bottle of pink champagne and chocolate truffles. She stole one immediately.

'I haven't stopped, not even for lunch,' she said, explaining her urgent desire of a chocolate treat.

'Put the kettle on for tea while I set up the cupcakes.'

She filled the kettle, put it on to boil, and glanced over at Struan who was setting plain cupcakes out on a large white plate. He lifted two icing bags complete with nozzles from the picnic hamper. 'Buttercream or strawberry icing?' He held them up, making her choose.

Lucy frowned.

He forced them closer. 'Come on. Are you better at adding buttercream or finishing the cupcakes with strawberry icing?'

She laughed. 'You want me to ice the cupcakes?'

'I thought the catering staff at the chateau would do it, or you could decorate them and maybe it would help with your creative ideas.'

She chose the buttercream. 'I'll add this. You can do the strawberry icing, but I get to add the sprinkles when we've finished.'

'Deal.'

She proceeded to make a complete mess with the buttercream. 'These nozzles have a mind of their own.'

'You're applying uneven pressure. Keep it smooth and light.' He took control of her hands and a tingle of excitement shot through her at his closeness, though she was certain he didn't mean to cause such a reaction. He seemed intent on showing her the best method for creating swirls of buttercream on the cupcakes. He even let her try her hand at the strawberry icing. She wasn't very adept at that either, though perhaps she would have been if it wasn't for the adrenalin pumping through her system whenever she felt the warmth of his body so close to hers. Her hands shook, making wobbly and wild splashes of icing.

He finished icing the cupcakes, smoothing over the mess she'd made. Then he handed her the sprinkles.

'This I can do,' she said, and added the colourful sprinkles on to the cupcakes.

'Perfect,' he announced.

'Far from perfect,' she corrected him.

'This is my day for telling little white lies,' he said in his defence.

She looked at the shameful state of the cupcakes. 'That's a whopper of a lie.'

He took a tissue and wiped a smudge of buttercream off her cheek, an action which seemed far more personal than it really was. There was something intimate about it, about Struan, she thought, and felt the colour burst across her cheeks.

If he noticed, he didn't say anything. Instead he popped open the champagne and poured them two glasses.

'So much for the ginger beer and lemonade lifestyle.' She tipped her glass against his and drank the bubbling pink liquid.

'One of those days for both of us. Tomorrow we return to being our safe selves again.'

He tipped his glass against hers after refilling them.

'Agreed.' She smiled at him and realised that she felt — happy.

The rawness of the emotion took her aback. Her reaction showed on her face.

'Are you okay, Lucy?' He gazed down at her with those gorgeous blue eyes, causing all sorts of reactions within her.

'Yes, I just. . . ' She hesitated. 'I know it sounds silly, but for a moment I totally forgot about work, about the deadline, about not being the Lucy you wanted.' She took a deep breath. 'And I felt *happy*.'

'You sound as if that emotion is alien to you.'

'Maybe it has been for a while. My world is work, more work, and for relaxation, thinking about work.'

'That's no way to live, Lucy. Though I'm not one to talk. The chateau is my entire universe and has been for several years since I inherited it from my parents. It'll continue to be like this for the foreseeable future.'

'We're two successful lost causes.'

He looked at his glass and then questioningly at her. 'Should we drink to that?'

'I'm not sure.'

16

'Neither am I.'

She looked at him, standing there so close to her, so tall and manly, yet somehow vulnerable, and realised how comfortable she felt with this man who was a virtual stranger.

'Let's eat the cupcakes,' she suggested.

The kettle boiled and they fell into easy step with each other making the tea. She set out the cups, while he took control of pouring the boiling water and refilling the kettle. They both added milk and sat down at the kitchen table to enjoy the afternoon tea treats.

She bit into one of the dainty cream cheese and tomato sandwiches. 'These are scrumptious.'

He mumbled his agreement.

'You seem to be as hungry as me,' she commented.

'I haven't had anything since our liquid breakfast.'

'Bret and Marcia keeping you busy?'

'Non–stop. Had I known what I'd let myself in for, I'd never have invited them to film here. But it seemed such a brilliant opportunity for publicity for the chateau. When a film's made in any real location, and if the film is successful, it attracts loads of attention.'

Lucy smirked.

'You're doing that smirking thing.'

She shrugged. 'I'm just picturing you having to deal with the film stars. I understand you can't rely on gossip in the glossies, but allegedly, Sanderson and Charmaine are quite temperamental. He has a reputation for charming the ladies, so warn your staff to be aware of being chatted up by a rich, handsome and hugely successful film star.'

'That pitch will definitely put them off, I don't think.'

'And Charmaine — she is really attractive. Prepare to lose your heart.'

'I'm done with romance.'

'Unlucky in love?'

'I have no sense when it comes to dating women. Most are only interested in my wealth from the chateau. I never know when they're lying to me until I'm involved with them.' He drank the remainder of his champagne. 'No, I'm far better off concentrating on work and hoping that one day, if I'm lucky, I'll meet someone who likes me despite my faults.'

'Are your faults forgivable?'

He shrugged his broad shoulders. 'I'm up at dawn every morning, work all day until late at night. When would I ever have time for a proper relationship? Any woman would have to match my schedule and we'd need to work in harmony to be together, if that makes sense.'

Lucy nodded. 'It makes perfect sense.'

'You're the first woman who has ever agreed with me about that.' She saw the truth of this in the depths of his eyes. The artist in her decided they were beautiful cerulean blue, and her heart ached a little just looking at him.

They ate more sandwiches, drank tea and laughed at the foolishness of their situation.

His firm lips curved into a sceptical grin. 'I'm hoping I'll look back on this time and be thankful I agreed to the movie scenes being filmed here.'

'Your chateau is going to be world renowned.'

'You're right of course,' he agreed.

'Sometimes, you've really got to take a chance on things.'

'Like you've done?'

'Yes,' she said quietly. 'When I drove here yesterday I imagined that today I'd be on my own, drawing and making headway with the book. And look at me — sitting here slightly tipsy, giddy from all the nonsense this morning, wondering what lies ahead at the party tonight which is sure to be a complete fiasco — and talking to a man I'm barely acquainted with as if I've known him forever.'

A surge of attraction shot between them. She was sure of it. So was he.

He stood up as if suddenly the intimacy of the kitchen was bearing down on him and he needed more room to breathe.

'Do you think I could have a peek at your illustrations?'

'Yes, but no tea or food near anything.' She wiped the remnants of chocolate truffle from her fingertips. 'I ban all messy stuff from my desk.'

He put everything down, wiped his hands and followed her through to the lounge. The glow from the snow outside shining through the window illuminated the room, as did the vintage lamps.

18

Copies of her two previous books lay on the table. He picked one up and flicked through it. 'You drew all of these illustrations by hand?'

'Yes.'

'How long does it take you?'

'Each illustration is designed per page. A page can take me hours to ink if I don't mess things up. Often I can illustrate two or three pages a day. If I work in the evenings I can manage more, or I use that time to tidy up any little blobs of ink from the petals and foliage.'

He touched the layout paper. 'This is extremely thin and smooth.'

She showed him the design she was working on. 'I use these pens, various sizes of nibs, with black ink to draw each design, every flower, every leaf. Once I've finished, I scan the illustration into my computer. Everything is hand–drawn, not computer generated, but I clean up any little mistakes or perhaps replace a flower with a butterfly to adjust the design.'

'It's a lot of work.'

'It is, but I enjoy it, and it's really quite relaxing working hard.'

He laughed.

'I've always enjoyed escaping into my own little world of creating art.'

'What happens after the design is as you want it?'

'It's added to the others and I build a page at a time until I have the entire book finished. Everything is emailed to my publishers. I also get to design the cover artwork.'

'And people colour in these illustrations?'

'They do.'

He flicked through the illustrations in her other book. 'They're exquisite.' He looked at her, and again she reacted to his closeness. 'Very beautiful.'

She stepped back, hoping he couldn't tell how much his manliness affected her. 'So that's it really. My world in a book.'

'I envy you.'

'Do you?'

'Here you are, far from home, still able to work. Although I love the chateau and miss it dearly any time I'm away, it's a fixed location. But you can work almost anywhere there's a desk and peace and quiet.' He lowered his head as if feeling guilty. 'I am sorry you've had no proper peace since you arrived. After the party this evening I promise you'll have all the time and solitude you require.'

'And use of the whirlpool?'

'Absolutely.'

He pointed to one of the illustrations. 'Are these tea roses?'

'They are. I like all the old–fashioned and traditional flowers.' She reached over to flick the page of her book to show him other vintage floral designs. He did the same and as their fingertips brushed lightly she felt a surge of energy charge through her, as if she'd reached in and touched lightning in a bottle, that undeniable spark between two people.

She pulled back from his long elegant fingers and rubbed her hands together instinctively in an attempt to ground herself.

There was an intense pause, each of them waiting for the other to break the tension.

'Why are you here, Struan?' she asked gently.

'To have afternoon tea with you.' He wandered over to her desk, pacing like he'd done earlier.

'Why are you really here?'

He stopped and dropped his guard completely. 'To be honest with you, I'm not sure. Hiding probably.'

'From Bret and the film crew?'

'The crew arrived and have settled into their rooms without any fuss. Bret and Marcia are with them. Everyone is being plied with coffee and cake. They're waiting on the stars arriving later by helicopter. They've asked permission to land on the front lawn of the chateau.'

'Quite an entrance.'

He sighed heavily and ran an exasperated hand through his hair, pushing it back from his brow.

She smiled at him. 'No wonder you're hiding.'

He looked at her with such intensity. 'It's not like me. I'm not usually perturbed by the arrival of affluent or prestigious guests.' He paused and then said, 'Maybe I just wanted to hide here and be with you, even for a little while.'

Realising he'd said too much, he hurried through to the kitchen and proceeded to pack the hamper with the remnants of their afternoon tea. 'I'll leave the rest of the chocolate truffles here.'

'They're delicious. Thank you for bringing me afternoon tea.'

He lifted the hamper and gazed at her. 'No, thank you for letting me take up so much of your time.'

She watched him walk away towards the chateau. His cream Aran knit jumper blended into the snow, while his dark hair and black cords were in stark contrast. And something changed inside her, though she wasn't quite sure what, or why she felt differently about where she was, in the cottage, so far from home.

CHAPTER THREE

Lucy Fantastic

Lucy sat down at her desk and concentrated on her artwork. The daisy and butterfly design was starting to take shape.

An hour passed without her really noticing the time. The desk lamp with its daylight bulb ensured a constant glow, enabling her to work even as the afternoon became early evening.

The whirring sound of a helicopter circling overheard made her run to the window and gaze out towards the chateau that was all lit up in the frosty twilight. She cupped her hand against the window. Was that Struan running towards the cottage?

She hurried to the door and saw him sprint across the garden.

'Lucy, hurry up. The stars are about to land.'

'Yes, but—'

'Please come with me to meet them. Ten minutes.'

'I'm not dressed to meet film stars.'

'You look wonderful. Jump into a pair of boots and let's go.'

Keeping her thick socks on, she stepped into her boots that were in the hallway near the front door. She threw her scarf on and hurried outside. The freezing air filled her lungs and felt a lot colder than the previous night. She started to trudge through the dense snow, following Struan who was making brisk progress towards the chateau.

She stumbled into a rut, and Struan scooped her up as he'd done that morning and ran with her over his shoulder.

Another memory for the archives she thought, though who would believe her? The night a tall, handsome man ran with her across the snow to meet two famous movie stars arriving by helicopter in the wilds of Scotland.

'We're nearly there, Lucy.'

'Where have I heard that before?' she shouted from her upside down position.

He laughed.

'Stop laughing, Struan. They'll think we're enjoying ourselves.'

'Aren't we?' He laughed again, and by now they'd reached the front entrance of the chateau where he placed her down carefully.

Bret applauded. 'I'm impressed, Lucy. I love a woman who is up for fun.'

Marcia stood back, glaring, arms folded, beside some of the film crew who'd gathered to welcome Sanderson and Charmaine. Even from this distance Lucy could feel the critical appraisal of her messy ponytail and unfashionable attire.

The gust from the helicopter landing sent a flurry of snowflakes into the cold night air.

Sanderson jumped out and bounded across towards Bret, leaving Charmaine to totter in his wake. Crew members ran to help her and unload their luggage before the pilot took off again.

Bret wrapped Sanderson in a manly hug. 'Glad you're here. You're in time for the party.' He introduced Struan to the actor. 'This is Struan, the owner of the chateau. He's been great. Very welcoming to us.'

Sanderson smiled, gave Struan a strong handshake and then hurried into the chateau out of the cold.

'We'll have plenty of time to chat at the party,' said Bret, excusing Sanderson's curt behaviour, especially as Lucy hadn't even been introduced. Then he looked thoughtful at Struan. 'I knew you reminded me of someone. In the right light, from a flattering angle, with good makeup and excellent photography, you could pass for a poor substitute for Sanderson.'

Marcia nodded and looked at Struan, as if seeing him for the first time. 'He could, couldn't he?'

Bret continued, 'Struan's got the height and the build. They're both around six–three with a lean–muscled physique.'

'Sanderson works at it,' Marcia said snippily. 'It doesn't come naturally.'

'I don't work out at all,' Struan admitted. 'I just run around all day and night. Keeping the chateau ticking over is a full–time task.'

'What about you, Lucy? You're in great shape for an ordinary person. What works for you?' Bret asked.

'Harassment. It keeps my system fired up.'

Bret laughed. 'You certainly look well on it. Glowing skin, shiny silky hair.'

23

Struan guffawed. 'Huh! You should see her hair when she gets out of bed in the morning.'

Bret looked disappointed. 'Ah, so you're together. I thought you were unattached Lucy.'

'I am. Struan and I have never been involved and we've no intention of doing so.'

Bret brightened. 'I'm pleased to hear it.'

Lucy wondered if she'd made a mistake. 'But I'm not looking for romance. I'm totally focussed on work.'

'No time for other indulgences?' Bret queried.

'None,' she said.

'Except for indulging in midnight relaxation in our exclusive whirlpool,' said Struan.

Bret's interest perked up. 'You have one of those? I didn't see it listed.'

'Yes, it's in our fitness suite, but Lucy has it all to herself at midnight. She hasn't indulged yet, but she's going to. She works hard and it's to help her think up new designs.'

'Designs?' said Bret.

'I illustrate colouring books.'

Bret smiled at her. 'Is there no end to your talents young lady?'

'She's rubbish at icing cupcakes,' Struan blurted out.

Bret was still thinking about the whirlpool. 'The pool could be useful. We'll include it in the scene where Charmaine tries to entice Sanderson after he tells her they're finished.'

'That would be so atmospheric,' said Marcia. 'I'll take some shots to send to the studio executives for approval. I bet they'll love it.'

'Does everything need approval?' Lucy asked Bret.

'Making movies is a complicated business. Millions of dollars are involved. With heavy investment, everything has to be agreed upon, though I'm given fairly free rein to create my vision.'

'Anything that gives a legitimate reason for the stars to show their assets is advantageous.' Marcia smirked. 'Who wouldn't want to see Sanderson with his shirt off?'

Lucy agreed. 'Oh yes — light golden tanned physique, honed, toned and rippling muscles.'

Struan glared at her. Was that a flicker of jealousy in his eyes?

Struan looked around. 'Where's Charmaine?'

24

'She went inside,' a crew member said.

'You may not actually meet Charmaine up close and personal,' Marcia told Struan. 'She's totally exclusive. But you will be allowed to smile and admire her from a distance.'

'I can hardly wait.'

'Shall we all go in?' Bret spread his arms to usher them inside.

Lucy remained where she was. 'You go ahead, I'm not properly dressed. I'll go get changed and see you at the party.'

'Okay,' Bret said to Lucy. 'And I got your email. Great press release. Better than I'd hoped for. I've forwarded a copy to the studio and one to Struan.'

'I'll make sure to read it later,' said Struan. 'I haven't had time to check my emails.'

Bret and Marcia went inside, leaving Struan with Lucy.

'I feel I've wasted more of your time, Lucy. I thought you'd like to meet the movie stars.'

'I've never been the star–struck type, but having watched a few of Sanderson's films, of course I was intrigued to see him. But other things have always impressed me more than stardom.'

'Such as?'

'Loyalty. A practical nature. A man who can be content with things. Someone who has a warm–hearted soul.'

Struan wondered if he ticked any of those boxes. He certainly hoped so.

'Of course,' she added, 'it helps if he's totally gorgeous.'

Struan was still smiling at her when his all–round hotel assistant, Heckie, a sturdy man in his fifties, came running out of the chateau towards them.

'Excuse me, Struan, the visitors are becoming restless. Shall I break out the eggnog?'

'Eh, yes. And tell them I'll be right through to join them.'

'I'll let you get on with things,' Lucy said to Struan.

'You're still coming to the party though, aren't you?'

'Yes, if only to smirk when you have a chance to admire Charmaine from afar.'

She could still hear him laugh as she hurried back to the cottage.

Lucy had packed one party dress, in case of an invitation emergency. She'd had no plans to join in the chateau's nightly entertainment and festivities, preferring to hunker down in the cottage and work. However, she'd thrown in a little red cocktail dress, a sparkling sequin and chiffon number that was so sheer it took up minimum space in her luggage, along with a pair of high–heeled shoes embellished with diamante.

So that's what she chose to wear to the party. She brushed her hair smooth and silky and added a diamante clasp, then made her way to the chateau. She wore boots and carried her heels.

'Is there anywhere I can leave my boots?' she whispered to Brona in the chateau foyer.

'There's a cloakroom behind the main desk. I'll take them for you, Lucy, and your jacket.'

Lucy slipped off her warm jacket, feeling suddenly vulnerable and exposed, even though she could see into the function room where the party was being held and many women were wearing figure–hugging dresses. She reasoned with herself that it was because she hadn't been out on the party scene since she'd broken up with her last boyfriend almost two years ago. Had it really been that long since she'd worn anything other than sensible, comfy clothing? She estimated it had. They split up the first week of December after a huge row about her refusal to ditch her book deadline and spend Christmas and New Year at his townhouse.

'You look a treat, Lucy,' said Brona. 'That's a lovely wee dress.'

'It certainly is,' a voice said over her shoulder.

Lucy turned to see Struan smiling at her. He wore a dark suit, shirt and tie. She wasn't sure if he looked more handsome in his Aran jumper or whether the suit was the reason her heart squeezed when she saw him.

Brona smiled to herself and left them standing together in the centre of the foyer. Other guests, some part of the film party and chateau clientele, milled around, but Lucy didn't notice them. Only Struan, standing there, unaware of the effect he had on her.

'You look wonderful, Lucy.'

She smiled up at him.

Marcia came marching over. Like many of the women, she wore a classy black evening dress. She eyed Lucy up and down. 'You're wearing a red dress.' Her tone was filled with accusation.

'Is there something wrong with my dress?'

'Yes, Charmaine is wearing a red dress this evening. She won't be happy.'

Charmaine was ensconced in the far corner of the party room. Her glossy, dark hair was swept up in a severe chignon. Unsmiling red lips matched the colour of her dress.

Struan peered over at her. 'Charmaine's dress looks like dull red satin, though it's hard to tell from this distance. Lucy's dress is sparkling. No one will think they're wearing something similar.'

Inside, Lucy was cheering Struan's bluntness.

Marcia marched away.

Lucy looked around. 'I haven't really seen how beautiful the chateau is except from an upside down vantage point.' She gazed around at the elegant foyer with its gold–coloured carpet, airy interior and sweeping staircase. She'd seen the breakfast room, but in the evening the chateau's white walls and chandelier lighting created an atmosphere that was indeed fit for a Hollywood movie.

'I'd be happy to give you a tour.'

'Shouldn't we show face at the party?'

He sighed heavily. 'We should. Another time perhaps? I'm putting up the Christmas tree tomorrow morning. Pop over for breakfast, if you have time.'

She acknowledged his offer but made no promises.

They headed into the party.

Bret saw them and waved them over. A staff member waylaid Struan, leaving Bret to chat to Lucy. 'Come on, I'll introduce you to Sanderson.' He looked around. 'He was here a minute ago.'

'Have you worked with Sanderson before?' said Lucy.

'Yes, this is our third movie.' Bret reeled off the titles of the films. Lucy knew them well.

'Unfortunately, I've rarely paid attention to who directs a film,' she admitted.

'Most people know the stars, but few could name the directors or producers of a movie. To tell you the truth, I prefer being anonymous. I enjoy this business, but I like my privacy. I can go about and no one recognises me.' A waiter offered them champagne. Bret lifted two glasses and handed one to Lucy. 'To us.'

She drank a toast with him.

'Sanderson wasn't my first choice for this particular movie,' he confessed. 'Neither was Charmaine.'

'Really? Who were your first choices?'

'Shaw Starlight and Tiara Timberlane.' He shrugged. 'But they were both tied up with shooting another movie. Our schedules clashed, so I offered the roles to Sanderson and Charmaine.'

'I love Shaw Starlight's films. He's an excellent actor. I think I've only seen one of Tiara Timberlane's films.'

'You enjoy going to the movies?'

'I do, though I tend to watch at home rather than going out to the cinema.'

'You'll attend our premiere of course?'

Lucy blinked. 'The premiere? A red carpet event?'

'Sure thing. We're having the usual opening night in Hollywood, then heading to London. Come to both, or either. Struan has promised to attend the one in London.'

'I'm tempted.'

He smiled at her. 'Excellent.'

From across the room he saw Sanderson and ushered her over to him. Sanderson wore an expensive suit. He looked and sounded like one of the leading characters he'd portrayed in his action–packed films. Sanderson's accent was similar to Bret's Los Angeles tone but was somewhat smoother.

Bret placed Lucy right in front of Sanderson.

'I want you to meet Lucy. She's fantastic.'

'Hi, come and dance with me, Lucy Fantastic.' Sanderson clasped her hand and led her on to the dance floor that was jumping with others enjoying the lively music. These people knew how to party.

Before she could refuse, not that she wanted to, and blushing profusely, Lucy found herself the centre of attention, dancing with Sanderson Sanders. It felt surreal. Another weird and wonderful memory to treasure — along with the realisation that Struan, Marcia and Charmaine were staring at her, all vying for the most surprised look on their faces.

'Why the heck is *she* dancing with Sanderson?' Marcia snapped at Bret.

Bret downed his champagne. 'Why the heck not?'

Lucy's intention to stay for an hour, maybe less, was cast aside in favour of partying with the Hollywood crowd and indulging in champagne cocktails.

During a brief breather from all the wild excitement and enticement to have just one more glass of bubbly, she told Sanderson how happy she was he was in the movie.

'I'm pleased that you got the part,' Lucy said to Sanderson. 'I like watching Shaw Starlight and Tiara Timberlane, but I think the chemistry between you and Charmaine will be terrific.'

Sanderson seemed unperturbed at the news he hadn't been first choice for the role. Charmaine overheard and her reaction could be heard throughout the function suite.

'Excuse me. Am I hearing right? I was second choice to. . . ' she could barely bring herself to utter the words, 'Tiara Timberlane?'

'Calm down Charmaine,' Sanderson told her.

'Don't tell me to calm down.' She pointed an accusing finger at Sanderson. 'Did you know about this?'

'Bret mentioned it weeks ago,' Sanderson admitted, sounding relaxed.

'He told you, but didn't tell me?' she shouted. 'Why am I the last to find out that I was second choice?'

Amid much screaming, accusations and borderline skirmishes, Charmaine stomped off to lock herself in her room, threatening not to have anything to do with Bret's stupid movie.

Bret glared at Lucy. 'You betrayed a confidence.'

'I didn't know it was a secret.'

'Everything is a secret in this business.'

'Perhaps I can placate Charmaine with chocolate fondue served in her room with fresh strawberries dipped in champagne?' Struan offered.

Bret shook his head. 'Anything less than diamonds won't work.'

Brona scurried off to the hotel kitchen, brewed up her special herb tea, set it on a silver tray and headed up the stairs to Charmaine's room.

Brona winked at Struan on passing. 'I'm taking Charmaine a wee cup of tea to settle her.' She gave him a knowing look and continued on her way.

Struan made no attempt to stop her. He was more concerned about Lucy. It was almost midnight and the former lemonade party girl was tipsy, overtired and in need of being taken safely to her cottage amid the blustery snowstorm swirling outside.

'Where did Brona put your boots?'

Lucy waved a carefree hand at Struan. 'I have no idea, but I don't need them. I can't dance in flurry boots.'

'Furry boots,' he corrected her.

'That's what I said.'

Sanderson was nowhere to be seen, which wasn't Struan's concern. Bret had fallen asleep in the corner and Marcia was attending to him.

Heckie came hurrying over. 'The snowstorm's getting worse, Struan. I've stoked the boilers with extra fuel and the back–up generators are on standby, so we're all sorted.'

'Thanks, Heckie.'

'Want a hand getting your wee lassie to the cottage?'

'I wouldn't mind. I can't find her boots.'

'They'll be in the cloakroom. I'll get them.'

Heckie came back with the boots and her jacket. 'She'll need more than this to keep her warm. It's roasting in here, but it'll freeze the bollocks off you outside.'

'A blanket. Bring a blanket while I get her jacket and boots on.'

He sat her down.

'No, Struan. I told you, I don't need my boots. I'm—'

'You've had too much to drink. I'm taking you to the cottage, but there's a blizzard outside.'

'You're throwing me outside in a blizzard? In this dress?'

'No, no. . . '

She started to sniffle. 'Yes you are. You're heartless. All men are.'

He somehow managed to put her jacket on her.

'Here's the blanket,' said Heckie. He looked at Lucy. 'Why is she crying? Have you upset her?'

'No, she's drunk and getting emotional.'

'Struan's throwing me out in the cold. He doesn't like me.' Her bottom lip trembled and her eyes welled–up.

Heckie tried not to laugh while unfolding the blanket and wrapping it around her.

'I do like you, Lucy,' Struan told her.

'No you don't. Just because you're rich and more handsome than Sanderson, doesn't mean you can cast me aside.' She sniffed and gave him a heart–melting look. 'You're using me. And I'm not even the right Lucy.'

Struan shook his head at Heckie, and together they wrapped her up in the blanket, put her boots on despite her protestations, and then Struan carried her outside.

CHAPTER FOUR

Cocktails and Chaos

Brona had set the tray down on a table in Charmaine's room — one of the luxury suites on the top floor of the chateau. Designer clothes and accessories were strewn around the room with Charmaine in the centre of it, still wearing her red dress, shoes kicked off, curled up on the chaise.

'I said I don't want herb tea,' Charmaine huffed.

Brona poured a cup of the golden liquid. 'It'll make you feel better — and it's great for your complexion.'

Charmaine glanced at the cup of tea. 'Is it?'

'Oh yes. You've got a lovely complexion, but after all the upset, even your eyes are a wee bit puffy.'

Charmaine got up and looked at herself in the dresser mirror. 'It's all Bret's fault, and Sanderson's.'

Brona folded Charmaine's clothes, hung them in the wardrobe and generally tidied up as she talked to her. 'That's men for you. Selfish swines. Struan's okay, as was my late husband, but most of them are bampots.'

Charmaine took a sip of tea. 'This tastes quite nice.'

'Drink it up. It'll soothe your frayed nerves. Nothing worse than having your nerves jangled when all you wanted to do was enjoy yourself at the party.'

Charmaine drank the tea while Brona continued. 'Mind you, men are easy to handle. They're not complicated creatures like us. Especially men like Bret.'

'I want nothing to do with his movie,' Charmaine complained. 'I'm flying back home to L.A. tomorrow.'

Brona shrugged her shoulders. 'Hmmm, you could, but it wouldn't be me if I was you. Particularly when you're the star of this film and Tiara whatever her name is, hasn't got a look in. Noooo, I'd act my socks off, show Bret and Sanderson how to raise the stakes when the game gets tough.'

Brona's pep talk along with the tea helped Charmaine make up her mind to stay and fight.

'We're filming one of the dramatic fight scenes tomorrow,' Charmaine explained. 'They'd all better be on their A–game.'

Brona put the empty teacup on the tray and got ready to leave. 'Heckie and some of the other staff have been told to give the balustrades on the staircase an extra polish so Sanderson can slide down it at speed. Does he always do his own stunts?'

Charmaine brushed her hair and got ready for bed. 'Most of the time.'

'What about you? Are you allowed a piece of the action?'

'No, the stunt fight coordinator has someone double for me when I'm supposed to punch Sanderson's character and fight him off.'

Brona blinked. 'What? They don't even let you take a punch at him? I bet you could manage that without hurting yourself. You're not made of porcelain, even though your skin looks a fair match for it.'

Charmaine smiled at the compliment. She stood up, clenched her fists and had a go at throwing a punch.

Brona stepped in to advise her. 'When you make a fist, keep your thumb on the outside so you don't damage your hand.' She gave a demonstration. Charmaine followed her lead. 'That's it, keep your fist tight, knuckles flat and put your shoulder into the punch. My father was a boxer. Many a right hook has come in handy for me since I was a young lassie. And here's how to follow through with an uppercut.'

By the time Brona left, Charmaine was ready to participate in the action scene. And not a single diamond had exchanged hands.

Struan set Lucy down in the lounge, took her boots off, replaced them with fluffy slippers to keep her feet warm, lit the log fire and put the kettle on for tea.

Lucy flopped like a rag doll on the sofa, still wrapped in the blanket, and watched the logs spark into flames, enjoying the cosiness of the cottage while the snow swirled past the window outside.

The fresh air had brought her to her senses, and she no longer thought Struan was casting her out into the freezing elements in her party frock.

'I shouldn't have had those cocktails,' she called through to him. 'Huge mistake. Never again.'

He continued to rattle around in the kitchen preparing tea and coffee. The aroma of coffee brewing wafted through to the lounge.

She propped herself up on the sofa cushions. 'I can't believe I was dancing with Sanderson. Marcia kept glaring at me. I wonder if there's something going on between her and Bret, or whether she fancies Sanderson? Not that I do.' She paused. 'If I paid you any unexpected compliments tonight, don't take them seriously. Blame the cocktails.' She paused again. 'I'm babbling, aren't I?'

He carried through a tray of tea and coffee and put it on a table beside the sofa. 'Drink your coffee.'

She lifted up the full mug of strong, black coffee. She wasn't a coffee drinker but knew it would help sober her up.

He sat on a chair beside the fire and drank tea. He'd taken his winter jacket off and wore his suit. She thought how suave and good looking he was, how the glow from the fire accentuated his handsome features.

'You're very quiet, Struan.'

He gazed at the fire. 'It's been quite a day and a night.'

'It has. It's hard to believe I only arrived here this time last night.'

'Clean slate tomorrow,' he said firmly. 'I won't ask you to get involved any further. It's too chaotic. I'm totally drained. I can't imagine how you must feel.'

'Drunk, dazed and discombobulated.'

He smiled but continued to gaze at the fire.

They were quiet for a moment.

'So you're putting the Christmas tree up tomorrow?' she said.

'Yes, I usually put it up on the first of December, but Bret asked me to wait until they'd arrived. He wants to film shots of it before the decorations are put on. He said they'd film it early tomorrow morning, so I plan to decorate it mid–morning after breakfast.'

'Am I still invited?'

'Don't feel obliged. As I said, I'm not going to ask you to give up any more of your time. You were right when you told me I couldn't turn the clock back and make up for the hours you'd lost. I'll not jeopardise your book deadline any further. Hopefully one day written–off won't have wasted your schedule.'

'No, and I did get some artwork done today.'

34

He let out a heavy sigh, and she couldn't help but feel sad. He was letting her go, which is what she'd wanted all day, but now. . . it made her feel empty, alone again.

He got up from the chair and took his cup through to the kitchen and washed it. He came back into the lounge and put his warm jacket on.

'You're leaving?' She couldn't hide the melancholy in her voice.

He nodded. 'Stand up for a moment.'

'What for?'

He took hold of her hands and pulled her to her feet. The blanket fell from around her and she stood there with the sequins on her dress scintillating in the firelight's glow.

'I want to make sure you're steady enough on your feet before I leave.'

She stood straight, showing him she was quite fine.

'Can you get yourself to bed?'

'Yes, I can manage.'

'Don't fall asleep on the sofa. Get a proper night's rest. Hopefully, you'll be reset in the morning and ready to get on with your illustrations.'

'I will.'

'I noticed you've very little milk and groceries left. I'll have Heckie drop some off in the morning. It's a service we provide for the holiday cottages, especially in the winter months. The nearest village with shops is a fair distance down the road.'

'Thanks.'

He headed out, insisting she stay in the lounge and keep warm.

'All the best with your book, Lucy.'

She heard the click of the front door as he left, and felt the gust of cold night air waft through.

He was gone, she thought, wrapping the blanket around her and listening to the crackling of the logs on the fire before going to bed.

Struan welcomed the walk back to the chateau. He didn't care about the blizzard. He'd always loved the winter. He loved Scotland, the seasons, the rain, Scotch mist across the heather–covered hills and long summer evenings when the twilight seemed to stretch forever. And he loved the snow. The chateau always looked its best set in a snowscape. The white architecture dazzled and it appeared more grand.

He blinked against the onslaught. Yes, he thought, this was the right location for Bret's film, and he planned to do his utmost to make things work.

He cast a glance back at Lucy's cottage. Lights still glowed from inside. He shouldn't have meddled with her livelihood, and yet. . . he was thankful he'd met her. If it hadn't been for all the nonsense of the day, he might never have known her. He trudged on and kicked the snow from his shoes at the entrance of chateau.

Heckie had ensured the party guests were shown to their rooms and the function suite cleared and tidied.

The night porter manned the reception desk. Heckie hung up the last set of keys and put his jacket on to leave.

'Did you get Lucy back safely?' Heckie asked Struan.

'I did. Could you make sure she gets an early morning delivery of milk and groceries?'

'I certainly will.' He dimmed the chandeliers to an evening glow in the foyer. 'Lucy's very nice, isn't she? I like her.'

'She is,' Struan agreed. 'Goodnight, Heckie.'

'Goodnight. See you in the morning for another dose of pandemonium.'

Struan went into his office.

'Are you heading to the lodge?' the night porter popped in to ask him. 'Or will I have someone turn down the bed in your room?'

'It's late. I'll stay here tonight, thanks.'

He checked his emails and read a copy of the press release Lucy had written. No wonder Bret had been pleased with it. It read well, making the film and the chateau sound enticing.

A stab of guilt shot through his heart. She'd done a damn fine job for two men she barely knew. If anything showed her character, it was her willingness to help them. Okay, so he'd sort of forced her to get involved, but she could've refused to go along with any of it, especially as he'd insulted her and made derogatory comments about her clothes.

Bret had repeatedly said at the party that Lucy was fantastic. Would the director make a play for her? Possibly. And if so, how did he feel about this?

'Your room's ready, Struan,' the porter said.

Struan flicked his computer off. 'Give me an early morning call. I don't want to sleep in.'

The porter made a note of it. 'Consider it done.'

From the window of his room Struan had a view of Lucy's cottage. The blizzard obscured the details but he saw the lights were still on. He took his jacket off, undid he tie and at that moment the lights went off.

Knowing she was okay, he went to bed, falling asleep with thoughts of her smiling and dancing in that sparkly little red dress.

Lucy couldn't settle. Several times she nodded off then jerked awake, thinking she was back home in her flat, and had to adjust to the cottage surroundings. This hadn't been an issue the previous night, but then she hadn't met Struan, or been partying with movie people, or drinking potent black coffee. The worst of it was the awful realisation that the thought of being back home made her anxious. Instead of feeling a sense of relief in familiar surroundings, she didn't want her trip to the cottage to be over. It was like having her world turned inside out.

At 3:30 a.m. she finally threw the covers back and got up out of bed.

Due to the cold night, she'd chosen to wear the cute Santa top and snowmen–print leggings her editor had given her. They were super snuggly. She stepped into her bootie–style slippers and padded through to the kitchen to make a cup of tea.

Opening the fridge, she saw that Struan was right about the lack of milk. There was only a dribble left, not enough to make a cuppa. She didn't like tea without milk and another black coffee was out of the question.

Sighing heavily, she went through to the lounge where the embers of the fire gave a welcoming glow. She sat on the rug in front of it, enjoying the warmth and comfort it provided. She'd always wanted to live in a house with a real log fire, but never had. Maybe if her book did well she'd buy herself a little cottage like this, away from the hustle and bustle.

She got up and looked out the patio doors. The blizzard had eased, leaving behind it drifts of fresh snow. Oh how tempting it was, for someone who loved the snow, to run out and make a snowman, or flop backwards into the soft landing of a drift. But she was far too sensible for that. Wasn't she?

She gazed out longingly and assured herself this wasn't like snow it the city that lasted only a few days before melting to slush. No, this was the start of the snow season at the chateau and lots more was guaranteed throughout December and especially in January. She had loads of time to make the most of it. And yet. . . it was tempting. . .

Without a cup of tea to settle her back to sleep, she wondered if a few deep breaths of fresh air would knock her out. The sensible thing would've been to open the lounge window. Instead she slid open the patio doors and stepped out. Her slipper boots sank into the soft snow, but the thickness of the knit fabric and fleecy lining kept her feet warm. The air was surprisingly still, reminding her of the previous night, when the cold had an energy to it, an exciting feeling.

She breathed in the freshness of the air, filling her lungs. Yes, this would help her sleep.

And there was the silence again. She'd miss this more than anything. She gazed up at the vast dark sky arching for miles above her. A scattering of stars trailed off in the distance.

Then it happened. . .

A sound behind her. The click of the patio doors closing and locking secure.

She ran over and tried to pry them open, but they were firmly shut, as were all the windows, the kitchen door and the front door. She'd locked it from inside before going to bed to make sure no one could get in. Unfortunately, this now included her.

She lifted the squirrel and checked up his crevice for a spare key. Nothing. She put him back down and considered her options, none of which were particularly appealing.

She could use the squirrel to break a window, reach in, open the latch and climb through. Nope, she couldn't do that. Or she could huddle beside the little evergreen at the front door for the next two hours until it was daylight, then walk up to the chateau at breakfast time and ask for a spare key. No, that wasn't a good idea either.

She decided she was going to have to make her way to the chateau right now. It wasn't that dark. The lights were on in the chateau foyer. The night porter or other staff would help with her predicament. Struan would never need to know about it.

Avoiding the ruts, she trudged through the snow towards the chateau. Again, it was one of those horribly exciting experiences she'd look back on and smile. If she hadn't been wearing a Santa top and snowmen leggings she'd have scored it higher than nine out of ten.

However, sophistication wasn't a priority. Reaching the chateau safely was.

The night porter saw her on the security monitor and hurried to the front entrance as she approached.

'Are you okay, Miss?' He sounded genuinely concerned.

'I've locked myself out of the cottage. It's—'

He scurried to the reception desk. 'Yes, I know which one it is, Lucy.' He unhooked a spare key, but before she could stop him, he pressed a buzzer asking for assistance. 'Someone will be right down to help you get back safe.'

'No, no I'm fine,' she insisted.

But it was too late. Help was on its way.

He fetched a shawl from the cloakroom. 'Put this round your shoulders. I'll have the kitchen porter make you a cup of tea.'

'I don't want to cause any fuss—'

'It's no problem. There's hardly a night goes by without some eejit, I mean, some guest needing assistance.'

The sound of someone running down the stairs made her look round. Struan, dressed in the bottom half of his pyjamas, came rushing down while trying to throw on his pyjama jacket.

'Struan!' She tried not to stare at his honed torso, the taut muscles of his chest and flat, toned abdominals.

Her stomach flipped. She hoped her reaction to his half–naked physique was due to the surprise of seeing him. But she knew she'd be lying.

'Lucy.' Blue eyes stared at her. 'I thought I'd left you tucked up in bed.'

The night porter's eyes widened, then he disguised this by feigning interest in the hotel register, scribbling something down, probably a note about her being an eejit.

'I wasn't in bed when you left, Struan,' she stated loud enough for the night porter to hear.

39

'Are you still drunk?' Struan asked, adding fuel to the fire of speculation.

Lucy put her hands on her hips. 'Do I look like I'm drunk?'

Struan's appraisal of her wasn't pretty. 'No, you look like you're dressed for a silly Santa sleepover.'

'You should talk,' she snapped at him. 'You're standing there half exposed, and those silk pyjamas are hiding very little of your. . . ' She flicked at glance at his manhood. The dark blue satin emphasized every angle of him.

He immediately held his jacket in front of his particulars.

Her stomach flipped again. The width of his shoulders and smooth skin sent palpitations through her to the core. Her cheeks flushed.

The kitchen porter wheeled through a tea trolley. 'This will heat you up,' he said cheerfully.

Struan frowned. 'But her cheeks are flushed.' He stepped closer and eyed her carefully. 'You're not coming down with a cold virus are you, Lucy?'

Her cheeks burned. 'No, I'm just feeling embarrassed and harassed.'

Struan gave a couple of covert signals to the porters. Lucy didn't know what it meant, but both of them melted into the background and left Struan alone to deal with Lucy.

A strong hand cupped her elbow. 'Come on. I'll take you to my room for some privacy and get you settled and calmed down.'

The thought of being with Struan in his room was the last thing to make her feel calm. But she hid her reaction. She disguised it well, even when they arrived and he sat her down on the edge of his bed and wrapped the shawl around her.

His gleaming torso was inches from her face.

Someone give me a gold star, she thought, for self–restraint and good behaviour in the presence of sheer and utter masculine temptation.

'Are you okay, Lucy? You've got a sort of faraway glazed look in your eyes.'

'Never felt better. At least, not for a long time.'

Phew! Was it getting hotter in here?

Struan sat down on the bed beside her, and in a well–meaning and caring gesture put a comforting arm around her and rubbed some heat into her shoulders.

She'd never swooned in her entire life, but there was always a first time for everything.

'Guests lock themselves out of the cottages all the time. The patio doors are a safety feature, but a bit of a hindrance if you don't know what buttons to press.'

Struan's closeness was pressing all her buttons.

'I'll bring the tea up. Relax until I come back.' He laid her down on his bed and covered her with a satin quilt.

That was the last thing she remembered until she woke up in his bed the next morning.

CHAPTER FIVE

Decorating the Christmas Tree

Struan's room had a small balcony. Lucy, realising she'd spent the night in Struan's bed, needed to breathe, to think. Had he joined her in bed? Had anything occurred between them?

She opened the balcony doors and stepped out. The cold air hit her, wakening her fully, but she still didn't know what had happened. The last thing she remembered was Struan leaving to get the tea, snuggling under the quilt and then. . . waking up.

'Good morning, Lucy.'

Lucy spun around as Brona entered with a breakfast tray.

Brona smiled cheerfully. 'How are you feeling after your wild night?'

'Wild night?' She sounded panicky.

'The party,' Brona clarified. 'All those cocktails.'

Lucy swept her hair back from her face. She didn't have a headache, thankfully. 'I'm fine, just a bit. . . unsettled. I can't quite remember everything from last night, especially being here.' She glanced at the bed.

Brona gave her a knowing nod and poured a cup of tea. 'You spent the night here on your own. Struan got you settled, and you went out like a light. I checked in on you while Struan showered and changed at home in his lodge. Then he started work at the crack of dawn. He's always been an early bird.'

'So we didn't. . . '

'Noooo. Struan would never take advantage anyway. He's trustworthy. A decent sort.'

The relief made Lucy smile, and she came over to drink the tea. Suddenly she had an appetite. The toast, fruit and fresh baked scone looked delicious.

'I'll have to leave you and get on. The film crew are buzzing around downstairs. It's so exciting.' Brona pointed to the bedside chair. 'We've put some of your clean clothes and boots there so you can walk back to the cottage without causing a distraction.'

Lucy laughed. 'My clothes are kind of eye–catching.'

'I'm a knitter, and some of my favourite cardigans are lovely–coloured Fair Isles and other bobble–textured knits.'

'I love knitting.'

'We've got a nice wee selection of local yarns in the craft shop downstairs. You should have a browse, and I've plenty of patterns if you need them.'

'The chateau has a craft shop?'

'Yes, and a boutique with some beautiful dresses and other clothes. A wee bitty expensive but worth a look.'

'Struan said he'd give me a tour of the chateau this morning.'

'You should take him up on his offer.'

'He's going to be busy decorating the tree and dealing with the film director.'

'I'm sure he'll make time for you, dear.' She gave Lucy a knowing smile.

Lucy smiled back.

'Right,' said Brona. 'I'll skedaddle and see you later. Struan says to use his shower and whatever else you need.'

'Thanks for the offer of knitting patterns,' Lucy called after her.

Brona waved and hurried away.

Lucy buttered the scone and ate it with her tea, along with a bowl of fresh fruit — strawberries, raspberries, grapes and diced melon.

Feeling fuelled up, she went through to the bathroom to shower. There was a handy array of hotel soaps and shampoo, but she saw Struan's personal toiletries in the cabinet. She shut the cabinet door, feeling she was spying on him. He'd had the decency to offer her the use of his room, so although she had the urge to snoop and perhaps sneak a peek inside his wardrobe and dressers to glean an insight into the man who had repeatedly come to her rescue, she refused to be tempted. He trusted her. She was the trustworthy type too.

Leaving everything as tidy as she found it, Lucy left Struan's room and went downstairs carrying her sleepover clothes in a bag.

Bret saw her coming down the stairs, but with her hair washed and dried smooth and shiny, and looking smartly dressed in a pair of charcoal trousers, white blouse and light grey cardigan, he'd no idea she'd slept at the chateau.

'Joining us for breakfast?'

'Thanks, Bret, but I've had breakfast and need to push on with the day's schedule.'

43

'Catch up with you later.' He smiled and went through to the breakfast room.

He passed Struan on the way.

Lucy lingered and listened.

'We've got all the footage we need of the Christmas tree,' Bret told him. 'So if you want to start decorating it, go ahead.'

'Great,' said Struan. 'It's going to be a busy day.'

'Certainly is. After breakfast we're filming some backdrop shots of the chateau. The snow looks fantastic. Then the crew will set up for Sanderson's first fight scene and the staircase stunt.'

'Guests have been informed and everyone's quite happy to accommodate the filming.' Struan took a piece of paper from his pocket. 'Here's a list of the names of those who have volunteered to be part of the background.'

Bret skimmed the list. 'Excellent. And is Heckie helping to bring the sleigh–ride round to the side of the chateau?'

'He is. It's all sorted. It's Heckie's brother who owns the stables, and he's explained about the horses being involved in Sanderson's stunt. Everyone's delighted. So it's all going according to plan. They're bringing a chestnut stallion and a dapple grey. Sanderson can see which one he prefers and gets along with, but they're both good–natured horses.'

Bret put his arm around Struan's shoulder. 'This is going to be great.'

Bret left and that's when Struan noticed Lucy loitering. She pretended to be interested in the craft shop which was tucked into a niche opposite the reception desk.

'Lucy,' Struan called to her.

She turned around. 'Struan.'

He strode over to her. 'You look bright and. . . lovely this morning.'

'Thanks to you, Brona and Heckie no doubt.'

He smiled and nodded, but there was something hesitant about him. And the way he looked at her as if. . . she couldn't figure it out.

He was classically dressed in a dark suit, white shirt and tie. Jeez, she thought, he was so stylish.

'I was wondering,' he began, tentatively, 'if I could possibly renege on something I said last night.'

She looked at him questioningly.

'I said I wouldn't ask you to get involved in things again, but. . . would you like to help me decorate the Christmas tree?'

'I'd love to.'

'Brilliant. Let's go through to the other lounge.' He stashed her bag behind the reception counter.

She followed him through and neither of them brought up the previous night's fiasco. She wanted to, but didn't know how to broach the subject of sleeping in his bed.

'Here it is,' Struan announced.

A real fir tree stood in a corner of the large lounge. Floor to ceiling windows with brocade drapes gave a view of the chateau's back garden. A fountain looked like it had been frozen in time. The water was solid and encrusted with snow crystals, as was everything else in the garden, reminding Lucy of a scene from a fantasy movie.

'I didn't realise the chateau had a garden like this.'

'I owe you a full tour — when you're not too busy.'

He lifted two large cardboard boxes from beside the doorway and brought them over to the tree.

'Shall we?' he said, opening them up.

Shiny baubles, ornaments galore and swathes of tinsel spilled from the boxes.

Lucy lifted one of the gold baubles, holding it in her hand, the size of a large apple, and saw her skewed reflection in it. Struan's reflection was there too — the first time she'd seen herself together with him. For a moment she was lost in thought.

'We'll put the fairy lights on first then decorate the branches with the baubles.'

She blinked from her wayward thoughts and held one end of the tangle of lights, helping him carefully unravel them.

'There are two sets of lights. We'll put the multi–coloured ones on first.'

Lucy helped wind the strands around the branches, distributing them as best she could.

'You're good at this,' he said.

'I've always loved decorating a Christmas tree.'

'With your family?'

'I've no family left.'

'Sorry, Lucy.'

'You weren't to know.' She continued adding the lights. 'What about you?'

'The same as you. I lost my mother several years ago. My father faded after she'd passed and he was gone a month later. They were always together.'

They were quiet for a moment, unravelling the second set of lights, both not wanting to dwell on difficulties from their pasts.

'I'll take an end while you climb up,' she said.

Struan stood on a step ladder and wrapped the lights around the tree top while Lucy dealt with the middle and lower branches.

Struan jumped down. 'Now hopefully they're working.' He pointed to the light switches. 'Flick them on and stand back in case they frazzle us.'

Lucy switched them on. No frazzling was involved. The tree glowed dazzling bright.

'Wow!' she said.

'Now for the baubles.'

They both reached into the same box, and his hand brushed against hers, once again sending tingles through her. She pulled her hand back and felt annoyed with herself that she was unable to hide her reaction, especially when the blush rose across her cheeks.

'I'm sorry, Lucy. I don't mean to embarrass you.'

'You don't embarrass me. You just. . . '

She hung a bauble on the tree and tried to focus on the decorations rather than his handsome features.

'Just what?'

'Nothing,' she snapped.

'No, it's not nothing. You should say what's bothering you.'

'I don't want to.'

'Why not?'

'Can we just leave it at that?'

She continued to hang the baubles while he toyed with a strand of tinsel.

'About last night. . . ' he began.

'I don't want to talk about it.' She dug out other ornaments from one of the boxes that included pine cones sprayed with gold and silver paint and sparkling glitter.

'It would be weird not to mention it. You slept in my bed last night. Surely we should talk. At least to get rid of the elephant in the room.'

'There's no elephant in the room, Struan. There's just a Christmas tree that I shouldn't even be decorating. I should be getting on with my own business instead of arguing with you over something that's never going to happen again.'

'So that's it? You're going to dismiss any feelings we could have for each other?'

'Right now, my feelings for you include seething rage, irritation and borderline throttling.' With a menacing look, she held up one of the large pine cones and squeezed it.

He guffawed. 'You're threatening me with a Christmas pine cone?'

'Don't tempt me,' she shouted. 'I've had a rough night.'

He gave her an incredulous look. '*You've* had a rough night?'

Lucy was still arguing with Struan when Bret came in.

'I don't give a flying f. . . fairytale about your pine cones, Struan. As far as I'm concerned you can stick them up your—'

'Ah, there you are, Lucy,' said Bret. 'I thought I heard you shouting. Is something wrong?'

Struan stepped in before she could reply. 'No, no, nothing wrong. Just squeals of delight when she saw the Christmas tree all lit up.' He glanced at her, hoping she'd go along with his excuse. He fussed with a bit of tinsel on the tree. 'Lucy has such good taste and I like to ask her advice about the festive decorations.'

'Yes, I was just telling Struan what to do with his sparkly pine cones.'

Struan glared at her and forced a smile.

'Such enthusiasm for your job,' Bret said to her. 'You should come and work for me in the New Year.'

'Did you hear that? I could go and work for Bret.'

Struan forced a smile. 'You could. Think about it.'

She gave Struan a defiant stare. 'I once thought about running away and joining the circus when I was eight, so never say never.'

Bret laughed. 'She's such a tease.'

'Isn't she.' Struan's jaw ached with the effort to grin.

Donnan stood at the door and cleared his throat. 'Eggnog is served in the front lounge.'

'Shall we go through?' Struan ushered them out.

He whispered anxiously to Lucy as they trailed behind Donnan and Bret. 'Behave yourself.'

CHAPTER SIX

Eggnog and a Punch–Up

Eggnog was being served to the film crew. Bret had insisted on drinking a toast with them before the day's filming.

Bret held up his glass. 'To great work, and great talent.'

The crew drank the toast, and then everyone started to set things up for the first shots of Sanderson and Charmaine. She sauntered in, draped in costume, looking like an ice princess, swathed in a velvet cloak with white faux fur trimmed hood. An icy breeze followed in her wake, then disappeared when Bret stepped forward, handed her a glass of eggnog and her carefully manicured hand accepted it. A truce. Things were back to normal.

'The horse–drawn sleigh is ready for you, Charmaine,' said Bret. 'We'll film you arriving at the chateau, then cut to the action with Sanderson.'

'I've been rethinking this scene — the action part where my character fights off Sanderson when he tries to lift her forcefully from the sleigh and carries her into the chateau.'

The happy atmosphere in the room flipped into the red zone. Lucy saw Bret's face tense.

'What part of the scene doesn't gel with you?' Bret asked Charmaine.

'I want to punch Sanderson in the face.' Charmaine cast a glance at Brona who was helping organise the eggnog. No one noticed the look that passed between the two women.

'Your character does that,' Bret said, not quite grasping what she meant.

Charmaine put her glass of eggnog down and made a fist. 'No, I want to throw the punch. Not a stunt double. Me.'

Bret's laughter broke the tension and several others laughed lightly, including Sanderson.

'But you'll hurt your hand, Charmaine, if you accidentally hit him,' said Bret.

'I won't. I'll miss him. Besides, I'm not made of porcelain. I ski every season. I swim in Hawaii. I fly halfway across the world to remote places like this,' she argued.

Sanderson gave Bret an easy–going smile. 'Let her do it. It'll be a hoot.'

Brona noticed Charmaine's fist tighten. A hoot indeed.

Bret spread his arms wide. 'Okay. Let's roll with it.' Then he whispered to Sanderson. 'We'll give her one take. She'll mess up, and then be happy for the punch double to stand in.' They smirked at each other, convinced their plan was set.

Charmaine swept past them, followed by wardrobe and makeup assistants. She passed by Brona.

'Give him the old one–two,' Brona advised her.

Charmaine gave Brona a furtive nod and continue on her way.

Lucy was torn between watching the forthcoming fiasco, or going to the cottage to begin work. The filming was about to start soon. She could always catch up with the bluebell drawings. Half an hour wasn't going to make a difference.

'Staying to watch?' Struan asked her.

'Maybe for a few minutes.'

'Are you still angry with me?'

She shook her head. 'But seeing Charmaine punch Sanderson, or pretend to, may help me vent my feelings.'

'A punch by proxy,' he said, smiling at her.

She laughed.

'Ah, there you are, Lucy,' said Bret. 'Would you like to take part in the first scene?'

She pointed to herself. 'Me?'

'Yeah, I'm looking for people to act casual, be part of the background. You're looking smart. How about it? Captured on film for all time.'

'What would I have to do? I've never acted before.'

'Just walk into the foyer, head over to reception, pick up your room keys, then mosey on up the staircase.'

'That sounds a lot more than being part of the background.' Not that she was complaining. In fact, she was tempted. She never thought it would appeal to her, to be part of the movie, but being offered a tiny role really excited her. Maybe it was her whole predicament? A broken night's sleep. Threatening Struan with a sparkly pine cone. Nothing in her normally well–ordered world was settled.

'Okay, I'll do it,' she heard herself say.

'Fantastic.'

Bret used that word a lot, she thought. Hopefully she'd live up to his high expectations.

With someone dabbing a power puff on her nose to reduce the glare, Lucy was placed where she needed to be at the chateau entrance. Bret should've told her it would be Struan who would hand her the keys. He'd become inveigled as well. She waved across at Struan, they exchanged a look and tried not to laugh.

Bret leaned close to Lucy. 'Keep the smirks in your pocket. This is a cool scene.'

Lucy ditched the grin. 'Got it.'

Bret went over to Struan and gave him instructions. Lucy watched Struan's reaction. Whatever Bret had asked him to do, Struan was reluctant. A few more words were bantered back and forth until finally Struan agreed to go along with Bret's plan.

Wardrobe assistants straightened Struan's tie, buttoned his jacket and brushed his hair back from his brow. A dab of powder to sort the nose glare and he was ready. As the assistants walked away, the sexy strands of hair tumbled down across his brow again. Lucy sighed, imagining what it would be like to run her fingers through them and smooth them back.

Lost in thoughts she'd no sense thinking, the start of the action scene caught her unawares. From his vantage point, Bret waved her to do as they'd agreed. The cameras were rolling and several other background volunteers played their part. Now it was time for Lucy to do her bit.

While she heard a kerfuffle outside and the sound of horses, Lucy walked up to the reception desk. Struan unhooked her room keys from the wall stand, but instead of handing them to her across the desk, he walked around, grasped her in a strong embrace and kissed her full on the lips.

Lucy swooned. Definitely swooned. Struan still held a possessive arm around her after their long and passionate kiss.

Behind them Sanderson marched in, carrying Charmaine who was struggling to escape from his manly clutches.

'Put me down,' Charmaine yelled at him. 'Get your filthy hands off me, you brute.'

The moment Sanderson unhanded her, Charmaine threw a punch at his face. Her knuckles connected with his jaw. She was supposed to miss, but got it wrong. Sanderson absorbed the punch and continued acting, unaware of the uppercut that was about to whack him.

Sanderson went down like a swatted bluebottle.

The crew looked to Bret for instruction. He wound his hand in the air, signalling them to keep rolling.

Moments later, Bret shouted, 'Okay, cut.'

Charmaine dusted off her knuckles. 'Will we do that take again, Bret?'

Brona, part of the background staff, gave Charmaine a furtive thumbs up.

Lucy's lips were still burning with the passion Struan had imprinted on them. In the surreal melee, she watched crew members haul Sanderson up to check he was okay.

'I'm fine,' Sanderson insisted, looking slightly dazed. Not wanting to look like a wuss, he smiled tightly at Charmaine. 'Good shot. You've got quite a right hook on you.'

'It was the uppercut that got you,' she corrected him proudly.

Bret was busy watching the replay, mentally crossing his fingers that they'd got this piece of gold dust in the can. He punched the air. 'We got it! Every bit of it. It's fantastic.'

'The horses are getting restless, Sir,' Heckie announced.

'We'll be right there,' Bret said and hurried out with the crew. 'Are you sure you can handle the horse scene?' he asked Sanderson.

A makeup assistant sprayed Sanderson's face with a misting of mineral water. Lucy wasn't sure if it was to simulate perspiration or calm the redness on his chin where he'd taken the whack.

'I'm good, Bret. Let's do this.' Sanderson clapped his hands, more to egg himself on than private applause.

'Can I hit him again?' Lucy heard Charmaine ask Bret as they left the foyer.

'No, once is enough,' said Bret. 'Those hits were star shots. They'll be highlights in the movie's trailer for sure.'

Charmaine was delighted.

'Can someone help clear the lighting in the foyer?' said Bret. 'I want minimum disruption to the hotel guests.'

Marcia, armed with a copy of the script, frowned at him. 'When did you start caring about causing people disruption?'

Bret blinked. 'You're right, Marcia. Tell the stunt coordinator to put the mats down at the bottom of the staircase. They can have a few practise runs while Sanderson deals with the horses.'

Bret and the others continued on, out of earshot of Lucy.

Struan stepped back behind the reception desk, putting a safe distance between him and Lucy, unsure what her reaction would be. She'd threatened him with pine cones for simply asking her to talk to him. What would she do now he'd kissed her?

Struan held his hands up in surrender. 'I'm sorry, Lucy. Bret wanted you to look surprised when I kissed you.'

'He could've warned me. I could've pretended to look surprised.'

'You told him you had no acting experience. He said too much was riding on getting the shot in one take to risk it on your reaction.'

She sighed. 'What have we got involved in? Why did he want us kissing in the background while Charmaine punches Sanderson's lights out? Surely the stars are the focus of the film.'

'Bret explained that all his films have deeper meanings woven into them. *Layers of storytelling* I think is the expression he used. This film has action and romance, so while Charmaine and Sanderson provided the action, he wanted us to enact the romance. We were the ying to their yang.' He frowned, wondering if he was explaining it the way Bret had told him.

'This is bizarre,' said Lucy.

'You're not angry with me?'

'No, I'm. . . ' She wasn't sure.

'Not drunk but dazed and discombobulated?' he suggested.

She nodded. 'Pretty much.'

'In a good way?'

'I'll need to think it about it.' She could still feel the sensation of his lips pressing against hers, claiming her, and the strength of his arms around her waist. He was so strong, but she knew this from how easily he'd thrown her over his shoulders — twice.

'Can I offer you a cup of tea?' said Struan.

'Yes, you can.'

'And cake?'

'Cake would be good.'

Donnan went by and Struan said, 'Could you bring Lucy tea and a slice of lemon drizzle cake? We'll be in the Christmas tree lounge.'

'Right away,' said Donnan.

'The lemon cake is light and won't spoil your appetite for lunch,' Struan told her.

'Lunch? Has the entire morning gone already?'

'No, it's still mid–morning.'

She relaxed slightly.

'I can have the tea and cake served in the cottage if you'd prefer.'

'No, I'll have it here and then get going. It's my own fault for being so starry–eyed about Bret wanting to include me in the film scene.'

'A once–in–a–lifetime offer.'

Lucy nodded. 'I couldn't resist. But I'll have a quick cuppa, and then I'll be ink deep in illustrating bluebells, butterflies and snowdrops.'

'Snowdrops on the art agenda today then?'

'They are.'

Lucy and Struan sat down at a table for two and she admired the Christmas tree.

She smiled as she gazed at it. 'It's lovely. No one would ever guess it was decorated amid our silly squabbles.'

'Couples do that at Christmastime. Tempers fray, especially when the fairy lights are in a fankle. But no one really means what they say. It's soon forgotten.'

Of all the things he'd said, the word *couples* resonated with her. They weren't a couple, and yet. . .

'I took the liberty of bringing you tea and a slice of your favourite chocolate cake,' Donnan said to Struan. He set a tray down on the table.

'Thank you, Donnan. I'm happy you did.'

They were chatting, and Struan was sharing a taste of his chocolate cake with Lucy when Bret came in.

'Just the couple I've been looking for.'

Lucy frowned at Struan. 'Should we run for the hills now, or finish our tea and cake first?'

Bret laughed.

'I think Bret's got us cornered again, Lucy.'

'I want a shot of the two of you at the Christmas tree while Sanderson runs through the lounge, chasing after Charmaine's ex–boyfriend, out through the patio doors and into the garden. We'll cut the shot after Sanderson dives into a snow drift, so keep gazing in each other's eyes romantically until I shout that we're done. I'm just filming a shot of Sanderson with one of the horses. Won't be long.'

Bret didn't wait for a response.

'Someone bring Struan and Lucy more cake,' Bret announced.

Donnan ran off to get it.

Lucy sipped her tea. 'Is life with you always this crazy?'

Before Struan could reply, Heckie came running into the lounge. His hair stood up in wild peaks. 'The horses are getting restless, Struan. Can we break out some of the fresh hay?'

Struan nodded and Heckie ran off again.

Lucy smiled. 'I'll take that as a yes.'

Marcia was helping Bret and Sanderson decide on the horse selection.

'The chestnut stallion gets my vote,' said Sanderson, patting the horse.

'He's a fine looking animal,' Bret acknowledged, 'but I wonder if the dapple grey blends better with the snowscape?'

'Why don't you use both horses?' Marcia suggested, stepping close to the stallion and the grey.

The horses whinnied and became restless whenever Marcia was near.

Brona stood beside Charmaine, holding up the edges of the velvet cape so it didn't get damp from the snow. They watched the horses' reaction to Marcia.

Brona whispered to Charmaine, 'Horses know about people. They just *know*.'

Charmaine nodded and pulled the hood of her cape up for warmth.

Sanderson settled into the saddle astride the chestnut stallion. Both man and beast were at ease with each other.

Heckie's brother had been given permission to take photographs of the actor and the horse.

Sanderson waved him over. 'Come and stand beside us. Give the camera to Heckie. Get some pics of you with us — and bring the grey into the shots.'

Heckie took charge of the camera and clicked off several shots of his brother standing proudly with Sanderson and the horses, proof that he'd been involved in the movie. The photos were to be kept private until filming was done. Assurances from Heckie and his brother were given and kept.

Brona pursed her lips and watched Sanderson. 'Sometimes I think he's a total arse, then he does something thoughtful and I think he's okay.'

'He is,' said Charmaine. 'I almost dated him last year.'

Brona adjusted her spectacles getting ready to hear the gossip. 'What happened?'

'Well. . . Sanderson was naked in my bubble bath helping me go over my lines. . . '

The movie's villain, the ex–boyfriend, paced up and down near the Christmas tree, never looking at Struan or Lucy as if they were invisible.

'He's getting into character,' said Bret. 'Don't disturb his vibe. He has to take himself into a dark place and find the ruthlessness of his character.'

'Fine by us,' said Struan.

Outside in the back garden, Sanderson was practising sprinting across the snow, seeing how quick he could go before the ruts slowed him down. Wardrobe had zipped him into a full bodysuit to prevent him ruining his costume — a dark suit, not unlike the one Struan was wearing.

'What do you want us to do?' Lucy asked Bret.

'The same as you did at reception. Show each other a little love. Let Struan kiss you. We want to feel the romance emanating from your souls.'

'Is that all?' Lucy said, smirking.

'Remember, Lucy, no smirking,' said Bret. 'Think romance, think giving in to his manly thrusting.'

Lucy almost choked on her tea. 'I beg your pardon?'

'The strength of him leaning forward, his heartfelt love, kissing you with passion, pulling you into his warm embrace. Think romance.'

Lucy let out a relieved breath. 'I thought you meant. Never mind. Sweet romance I can do.'

Marcia came tottering over. 'Sanderson wants to do a back–flip off the frozen fountain into a snow drift. Are we covered for that eventuality?'

'We are,' said Bret.

Marcia ticked the list on her clipboard and tottered away again.

Brona wiped the steam from her spectacles as Charmaine finished telling her about her involvement with Sanderson. 'Phew! That would make a great scene in itself.'

'So, as I'm sure you understand, I don't want anyone to find out about our almost romance.'

'My lips are sealed with sticky glue,' Brona assured Charmaine.

Charmaine smiled at her. 'It's so nice to have girlie chats with someone I can trust. I miss telling my mother. I used to confide in her.'

Brona assumed Charmaine's mother had passed away.

'No, she sold my secrets to the press to pay for her holidays in the Bahamas with her new boyfriend. We don't talk these days.'

'Perhaps in time you'll forgive her?' said Brona.

Charmaine shrugged. 'Ratting me out to the press — I can let that go. Business is business. But stealing my boyfriend from me?' She shook her head. 'I really liked that guy.'

Sanderson took another daring leap off the frozen fountain, landed in a snowdrift, then came bounding in out of the cold.

He unzipped himself in front of Lucy and Struan and stepped out of the bodysuit.

'I love that Christmas tree, Lucy,' Sanderson said as a wardrobe assistant straightened his shirt and tie.

And that's when Sanderson noticed something. 'Hey, Struan, we match. Our suits, shirts and ties are similar.' Then he joked, 'Maybe I should get you to double for me and jump off the fountain while I kiss Lucy Fantastic.'

'In a parallel universe, I might agree to do that,' said Struan.

Lucy joined in the light–hearted fun. 'Don't I get a say in this?'

Sanderson leaned close to her and gave her a devastating smile. 'Nope. You just get to break our hearts. Isn't that right, Struan?'

Struan looked at Lucy. 'Lucy is indeed a heart–breaker.'

Sanderson ran off to get ready for the scene, leaving Lucy wondering if Struan really did care about her.

'Get ready to roll, folks,' Bret announced.

Camera crew and others were all set. Heckie ensured the lounge doors were wide open to allow the actors a clear run through into the garden.

Struan and Lucy were given a quick dab of powder on their faces as they sat beside the Christmas tree.

Struan leaned close to Lucy across the table. 'I'm sorry, but I'll have to kiss you again, okay?'

Lucy nodded. The last time she'd been taken off–guard. She wondered how she'd react when he kissed her now. Think sweet romance, she told herself, trying not to blush as the adrenalin started hitting her system. The sheer thought of kissing Struan, perhaps for the last time, sent her senses into chaos.

Calm down. You can do this, she chided herself.

She'd been so intent in her own thoughts that she didn't hear Bret shout, 'Action.'

As the villainous character raced through the lounge, closely followed by Sanderson, she was taken aback when Struan leaned over the table and kissed her, long and hard, with passion, with warmth. Somehow, he'd surprised her again.

Although she was part of the background, she felt the complete opposite. In her bubble of passion with a man she truly did have feelings for, the background was Sanderson and his acrobatic antics in the garden. She thought she heard a round of applause for Sanderson's daring. He must have achieved a perfect landing in the snowdrift. But all she felt was Struan's firm lips kissing the breath out of her.

CHAPTER SEVEN

Sizzle Factor

Lucy needed to calm down. Telling Bret she'd had a great experience, she left the filming fiasco and headed to her cottage.

It was lunchtime and a warm, winter sun shone in the vibrant blue sky. She closed the door of the cottage and locked it. Locked out the entire world so she could settle herself.

She dumped her clothes bag on the bed and went through to the kitchen. The pretty yellow floral blind caught the sunlight and gave the kitchen a warm glow.

Heckie had stocked her fridge with milk, eggs, cheese and fresh vegetables. Tins of lentil soup and Scotch broth were stacked in the cupboards, and the biscuit barrel beside the tea caddy had been filled with a selection of chocolate digestives, custard creams and tea cakes. A packet of shortbread sat on the table where she couldn't miss it. She loved shortbread, but her tummy was still churning with an assortment of emotions.

She made tea and sat down at the kitchen table to gather her senses. Maybe if she didn't go near the chateau again everything would settle back into its original groove and she could get on with her illustrations as planned. Yes, she thought, that's what she needed to do. She had a plan and was going to stick to it.

Unfortunately, Marcia arrived to disrupt everything.

If it had been Struan or any of the others knocking on the door of the cottage, she would've pretended to be out or asleep. She'd have hidden inside until they'd gone. But this was Marcia. More cunning than all of them. Brona had confided to Lucy that even the horses didn't like Bret's wily assistant, and animals *knew* these things.

So when Marcia knocked, not on the front door, but on the kitchen window and waved through to her, Lucy was forced to open the kitchen door and let her in.

Marcia wore boots and a stylish business skirt suit. No sensible jacket. Not for Marcia who defied the cold conditions.

Marcia glared and then forced herself to say, 'Good news for you, Lucy. The studio saw the dailies, loved the chemistry between you and Struan, and want to offer you a contract.'

'A contract? For what?'

Marcia stepped inside. 'Sit down and let me explain.'

Lucy and Marcia sat down at the kitchen table. Lucy offered her tea. She refused.

'The studio executives are sent the movie's daily unedited footage by Bret. They give their feedback.'

Lucy nodded and listened.

'Bret sent them a preview and their reaction was immediate. They just phoned him.'

Lucy felt nervous and continued to listen.

'When the studio saw the dailies with you and Struan kissing in both scenes, they loved your onscreen chemistry together. Personally, I think you've got the hots for the guy but won't admit it. Anyway, we call it sizzle factor.'

'I'm not interested. I have floral illustrations to complete.'

'Excuse me — you'd rather draw roses and tulips than be part of a movie?'

Marcia's attitude rankled Lucy. 'The roses and tulips are drawn. I'm now working on the snowdrops.'

'Oh right, so you prefer to illustrate snowdrops than be a Hollywood player.'

Lucy went to protest, but Marcia cut–in. 'Let me tell you something. Whatever deal you have with your publishers, the studio will match it and notch it up a zone.'

'This is my career, Marcia.'

Marcia took out her phone. She held her hand up to silence Lucy. 'I'm phoning the studio.'

Lucy sat sipping her tea while Marcia spoke to them.

'Lucy's being difficult. She's holding up filming. She'll cost us millions of dollars in lost revenue.' She paused and listened. 'Yeah, okay, bye.'

Lucy put her cup down, wondering what the studio had said.

'They're offering to pay you double the fee. They pay big for sizzle factor.'

'But I—'

'Honey, I just got you the best deal of your life.'

60

Marcia stood up, unwilling to listen to Lucy's objections. She opened the kitchen door and stepped out. She glared again at Lucy. 'With the money you'll get, you'd be able to buy a cottage like this and still have plenty of cash in the bank.' She waited for a response from Lucy and on getting no further objections she snapped, 'You're welcome.'

Panic. Sheer panic. That was the one emotion burning through Lucy. She wanted to tell Marcia she wasn't doing it, and probably would have if it hadn't been for her parting shot. The thought of affording to buy a house, a cottage, was hard to turn down. She had to adjust her plan.

She phoned the chateau and asked to speak to Struan.

'Hello, Lucy. Are you okay?'

'You know that parallel universe you were talking about. . . '

Struan came down to the cottage to talk to Lucy.

'Marcia spoke to me too,' he said. 'Quite an offer they're making.'

'You don't need the money surely?'

'No. But someone in a lesser financial position would be silly to throw money like that away.' He looked right at her. 'I'm not trying to insult your career. I think what you've achieved is amazing. You're a talented artist. However, ask yourself — would you refuse the deal if you didn't have a book deadline?'

'Put like that, I suppose not, but I do have a deadline.'

'What if there was a way to fit both into your schedule, would you consider it?'

'Do you have a plan?'

'Sort of. When I first took over the chateau, I had to run around trying to check the bookings, deal with banking, marketing, management, staff hiring, advertising. There were days when it didn't seem feasible to do everything.'

'What did you do?'

'I had a phrase. Everything needs done. I can't do everything. But everything needs done.'

'You'll have to run that by me again. I don't get.'

He did. She still didn't get it.

'That's because I somehow managed to do everything despite it being crazy.'

'You really managed to do it?'

'You've seen the chateau. You're in one of the holiday cottages. I made it happen. I worked round the clock, napping and eating when I could. But for you, it would be different because I'd help you.'

'Why?'

'That's the wrong question, Lucy.'

She thought for a second and then said, 'How will you help me?'

He pointed at her. 'That's right. How?' He continued to explain. 'What if I provided you with back–up for the mundane — meals, groceries, making sure you don't get up to any midnight mischief wandering around in the snow in your jim–jams?'

She laughed.

'If I did that for you, and all you had to do was concentrate on your artwork, and a little bit of filming, could you do it?'

'Yes.'

He smiled.

'Now can I ask why?'

'Nope.' He turned her around and playfully marched her over to her desk. 'Start drawing snowdrops.'

She laughed as he went through to the kitchen, made her a cup of tea, served up with a piece of shortbread, and brought it through to the lounge.

'Don't spill it on your artwork,' he said. 'Staff will drop off your lunch and dinner. You'll have hours of uninterrupted drawing time.'

Struan left her to get on with it. And she did. Something in her clicked into efficiency mode. She couldn't wait to draw the snowdrops and bluebells and a smattering of little butterflies.

By the glow of her desk lamp she worked like mad.

The tea and shortbread was delicious. And she didn't mess up her artwork once.

The sun faded by late afternoon, but inside the cottage Lucy was cosy and warm. She'd put more logs on the fire in the lounge and flicked on other lamps as the day darkened.

Donnan dropped off a tasty lunch for her, stopping only to set up a plate of Scottish salmon and vegetables. She'd declined pudding, preferring to get on with her art.

'Sorry lunch is a bit late, and there are no carrots to go with your broccoli,' said Donnan. 'The catering staff had to remake the buffet for the film crew after one of the horses caused pandemonium in the chateau.'

Donnan sounded unperturbed and put a folded napkin down beside her cutlery, giving her the full silver service experience.

'Is everything okay?'

'Och, aye. After you left, Sanderson did his fight scene where he rode the chestnut stallion up to the front of the chateau. The director was happy and everyone was applauding, then Neddy decided to gallop into the foyer and cause a rumpus. He must've smelled the lunches being cooked. Lemon carrots were on the menu. Sanderson tried to rein him in, but he nosed his way into the kitchens. It took two chefs and Brona to get him out.' He sniggered. 'The horse, not the actor.'

'Where was Sanderson?'

'In the saddle the whole time. The horse really liked him.'

'What about Struan?'

'He did a better job. He was on the dapple grey.'

'Struan rode one of the horses?'

Donnan nodded.

'And I missed this?'

'You had wee flowers to draw.'

Pandemonium aside, Lucy wished she'd seen this.

Donnan smiled. 'But, as I say, everything ended okay, and the director has film footage of the horses he never thought feasible.' He spooned lemon butter sauce over her salmon. 'And few men suit a kilt quite like our Struan, even when going commando astride a horse.'

Lucy looked concerned. 'Where was Heckie?'

'Busy helping his brother tie Charmaine to the sleigh. I thought these fancy stars had doubles for the rough and tumble bits, but that lassie's been throwing herself about with the men all day.'

Donnan gave Lucy a cheery wave and left her to enjoy her lunch. She did, and then pushed on with her artwork, trying not to think about Struan in a kilt.

Two shorts tea breaks ensured Lucy had used her time well. She'd even sketched a squirrel, inspired by the ornamental one on the

63

doorstep, which she thought would suit an autumn–themed page of leaves, pumpkins and acorns.

She stretched and eased off the tension in her neck and back, happy with what she'd achieved.

Her phone rang. It was Struan.

'Am I interrupting?'

'No, I've just finished drawing fuchsias and a squirrel.'

'Bret wants to film some twilight shots of us. Any chance you could come up to the chateau and kiss me?'

She laughed. 'See you soon.'

Lucy tidied her hair, put on a Fair Isle jumper and walked up to the chateau. Brona mentioning about Fair Isle knitting put her in the notion to wear it. She still wore the grey trousers and white blouse, so if Bret wanted something less colourful, she could take the jumper off. The main palette of the jumper was grey, so it toned with her trousers, but the hues included indigo, madder and yellow.

She walked briskly through the snow, enjoying the cold fresh air. The white chateau sparkled in the early evening light, and broad bands of vibrant pinks and purples stretched across the sky, casting a warm glow on the building.

On the second floor balcony, Struan's room if she wasn't mistaken, people were milling around. Yes, there was Struan and Bret on the balcony. She hurried on not wishing to be late.

'The film people are up in Struan's room,' Brona told her in the foyer.

Lucy ran up the stairs.

'I like your Fair Isle, Lucy,' Brona called after her.

Lucy turned, gave her a quick wave, and then ran on.

Bret was pleased to see her walk into the room. 'I'm delighted you're going to continue to be part of the movie, Lucy.'

'I've emailed copies of the contracts to Struan,' said Marcia. 'He can give you your copy. Sign them and then email them back to me.'

'I will,' said Lucy.

Struan took her aside for a moment. He kept his voice down. 'I've read over the contracts and they're extremely generous. I ran them past my lawyer. He said they're straightforward and contain no spurious clauses.'

'Great, we'll sign them later.'

'Lucy, could you stand on the balcony?' said Bret.

She went over and stood there. The sky behind her was ablaze with colour in the Scottish twilight. 'Do you want me to take my jumper off?'

Bret peered through one of the cameras, trying to angle the shots he had in mind. 'No, keep your clothes on.'

'That's not what I was meaning,' she said, but no one was listening. Everyone was busy with their own tasks, getting ready to capture the twilight before it faded to night.

'Struan, stand beside Lucy,' Bret instructed. 'When I give you the signal, I want you to do what we were talking about.'

'What was that?' asked Lucy.

'We're looking for romantic smouldering,' said Bret. 'I'll cut this in with the main scene, so don't worry about anything being out of situ. It'll all make sense in the final editing. It's part of a montage featuring Sanderson and Charmaine.'

Lucy took a calming breath.

'Okay, folks,' said Bret. 'Action.'

Struan lifted Lucy up in his arms and kissed her. Lucy instinctively touched his face, showing that she welcomed his kiss. This was true. Kissing Struan could become a hobby of hers.

'Cut,' shouted Bret.

Struan stopped kissing her and put her down gently.

Bret ran the playback. He sounded happy with the effect of the twilight background. 'I got what we need, folks. Let's move on to the next shot.'

Lucy pressed her cold hands against her burning cheeks and glanced at Struan. 'I'm blushing again. You're lucky it doesn't affect you like this.'

'Inside, I'm blushing like mad,' Struan confessed.

'You're just saying that to make me feel better.'

Struan opened his jacket, took her hand and pressed it against the white fabric of his shirt. 'Feel my heart.'

Lucy's fingers felt the sinewy muscles of his chest and the thunderous beat of a strong heart.

Her pale grey eyes looked up at him. No words necessary. She pulled her hand away and he buttoned his jacket.

Everyone headed downstairs.

While the lighting crew set up the next shot, which was in the lounge with the Christmas tree and a view of the garden, Struan spoke to Lucy about her art.

'You drew a squirrel?'

'It's for an autumnal design. I've never drawn a squirrel before, but he fits in well with the acorns illustration.'

'There is a lot more to your colouring book work than I first thought. I've ordered copies of your books for the chateau's craft shop.'

'You've bought my books?'

'Yes, I placed an online order for them today.'

She smiled. 'I didn't expect you to do that, Struan.'

'And I was wondering. . . I've been wanting vintage–style botanical prints to frame and put up in the holiday cottages.'

'I'd be happy to give you some of my artwork.'

He shook his head. 'I'd buy it.'

'Yes, but I'd—'

'That's settled. And one more thing. Do you by any chance create larger artwork, something suitable for the foyer wall?'

'I do. I draw substantial–sized illustrations, and some are hanging up in restaurants and tearooms. I also paint if you'd prefer watercolour or acrylics.'

'I like the sound of all of these. I've wanted paintings for the chateau, but haven't had time to trawl art galleries, so to have an artist on my doorstep seems like a great opportunity.'

'I have a portfolio of my illustrations with me, and I have a website where you can browse my artwork.'

'Perfect.'

'Does anyone in wardrobe have a suitable evening dress for Lucy to wear?' Bret asked.

Marcie spoke up. 'No one was prepared for a Lucy. It'll take a couple of days in these weather conditions to get costume additions flown up.'

'There are some smashing dresses in our boutique,' Brona suggested.

'Lead the way,' Bret said to Brona.

Lucy looked at Struan. 'Did Bret say anything to you about me wearing an evening dress?'

'He mentioned something briefly, but he has a tendency to flit from one topic to the next.'

'Come on, Lucy,' Bret beckoned her.

The boutique was beside the craft shop. Two clothes rails dripped with designer dresses, some cocktail–style, others full–length. Bret flicked through them, looking like a man who was experienced in choosing fashion wear. 'Lucy, try this on.' He handed her a silver sequin gown.

Lucy took it into the tiny changing room and slipped it on. It fitted quite well, perhaps a bit loose around the hips, but because of the fabric's texture, it looked fine. She tightened the adjustable shoestring straps. Yes, she thought, this was quite lovely.

Bret handed in another dress, a gold number, similar in style to the silver. He had a peek at the silver one she was wearing and nodded his approval.

'Try the gold, just in case it's more scintillating.'

Brona helped him sort through accessories. 'These shoes are nice. They'd go well with either of the dresses.'

Bret liked the shoes. 'What's your shoe size, Lucy?' he called through to her.

She told him and he changed them for a better fit.

Brona selected an evening bag, a sequin clutch. Bret approved of it too.

Lucy stepped out wearing the gold dress.

Bret gave it a thumbs–up. 'We'll take both dresses. Keep the gold dress on.'

Brona checked the price label on the silver dress and gasped.

Bret looked at it. 'Very reasonable. We'll take all these items.'

Brona whispered to Lucy. 'It's another world, isn't it?'

Struan joined them. 'Find what you needed?'

'Yes,' said Bret, 'doesn't Lucy look cute?'

Struan's expression showed she looked more than cute. 'She certainly does.'

Bret led them back through to the lounge. Sanderson stood beside the Christmas tree. He wore a suit, and someone was combing his hair.

'I want you to dance with Sanderson the way you were dancing last night, Lucy,' said Bret.

She frowned. 'Dance with Sanderson? Not with Struan?'

'The montage will merge with a couple of flashbacks,' Bret explained. 'It'll work better if I have shots of you and Sanderson together kissing.'

Struan sounded annoyed. 'You want Lucy to kiss Sanderson?'

'Exactly. Then I'll put the whole vision together in the romantic snowscape montage.' Bret sounded like he knew precisely how the finished scenes would look.

'Bret knows what he's doing,' said Marcia. 'No one envisions quite like Bret. You'll love what he does with this. Everyone always does.'

Struan wasn't happy. 'From reading the script, I can't imagine how this fits in.'

'People never do,' Marcia snapped, annoyed at Struan for questioning Bret's artistic ability.

'I've worked with Bret before,' said Sanderson. 'I never know what we're doing until I see what we've done.'

'Struan, I want you to stand in the background looking menacing,' said Bret.

This wasn't a stretch for Struan. Seeing Lucy in Sanderson's arms adversely affected him.

'That's perfect,' said Bret. 'Okay, cue music and. . . action.'

Lucy danced with Sanderson. They slow–danced in front of the Christmas tree. Jealousy burned through Struan and he did something underhand, hoping to break the moment. While the camera focussed on Lucy and Sanderson, Struan signalled to Heckie to press a button on the sound system. The music changed to an upbeat tempo.

Bret waved to keep the cameras rolling and continued to film Sanderson loosening his tie and getting into the party vibe. Lucy joined in, and danced as she had the previous night, only this time she was sober.

As the song drew to a close, Sanderson pulled Lucy into his embrace and kissed her.

Struan could barely watch. When the music stopped he walked out into the snow to cool his anger.

Sanderson didn't even notice. 'How did we look together, Bret? Great, huh?'

Bret was watching the playback with an unsure expression. 'Yeah, you and Lucy sizzle, but I'd like you to do it again with her wearing the silver dress. I think the gold dazzles and clashes with the tree decorations. Go put on the silver dress, Lucy.'

Lucy hurried out of the lounge with Brona who helped her change dresses in the boutique.

They heard Struan arguing with Bret. 'You want her to kiss Sanderson again? What difference does the dress make? Gold or silver — they're both sparkly.'

'Calm down, Struan,' said Sanderson. 'I'm not making a move on your girlfriend. This is just movie–making, buddy.'

'Lucy is not my girlfriend,' Struan shouted.

Sanderson sounded calm. 'Great, then we're all good.'

Struan stopped objecting, feeling everyone watching him. He shook his head, angry with himself. It had been a long day, and he'd been kissing Lucy a lot. Who could blame him for overreacting?

Lucy came back wearing the sparkling silver dress.

'Hit the music again, Heckie,' said Bret.

Lucy and Sanderson danced and smooched again to the upbeat rhythm while Struan stood in the background looking more dejected than menacing. When it came to romance, he was never lucky.

CHAPTER EIGHT

Flowers and Bumblebees

Kissing Sanderson felt awkward. Most women would've loved to smooch and dance with him, and although he was a great kisser, she preferred Struan. Thankfully, Bret liked the second dress and she didn't have to do the scene again.

Bret told her to keep the dresses and accessories. Filming was finished and Bret and the crew went through to the bar for a drink.

Lucy changed back into her normal clothes and put the dresses in a bag.

'Are you decent?' Struan called through to her in the boutique changing room.

'Yes, you can come in.'

They were alone in the confines of the boutique.

'You danced well with Sanderson,' he said. 'I apologise if I seemed to overreact.'

'It's been a stressful, surreal and weirdly sensational time.'

He relaxed his broad shoulders and smiled. 'It certainly has. I've no idea what we're going to look like in Bret's movie. Marcia said it may end up being like a dream sequence.'

'What's on the agenda for tomorrow?'

'Loads of work for you young lady. You'll be in your cottage drawing up a storm.'

'Sounds perfect. And speaking for storms, Brona says another blizzard is forecast.'

'There is. Be prepared to be snowed–in at the cottage. Imagine all the illustrations you'll get done.'

'Sanderson could dangle from a helicopter wire in a daring stunt to drop off my groceries,' she said.

'He could paraglide off the roof of the chateau and land in your front garden, Lucy.'

'He'd be daring enough to do it.'

'He would.'

She smirked. 'I thought perhaps you'd ride up on a horse, wearing your kilt, to deliver sustenance.'

'You heard about the fiasco?'

'Donnan told me. I'm sorry I missed it.'

'Bret asked me if I had a kilt. I keep one in my room at the chateau because we're always having a ceilidh. I thought he wanted to borrow it for Sanderson as we're similar in build. I didn't expect to have to wear it or participate in the horse scene.'

'Bret's artistic vision knows no bounds.'

Struan had a copy of the contracts with him. 'Do you want to sign the contracts so I can get them back to Marcia?'

'Yes, do you have a pen?'

He took a pen from his inside jacket pocket and handed it to her. She leaned on the boutique counter to sign her copy. He signed his.

Struan dimmed the lights in the boutique and tucked the contracts behind the reception desk while Lucy headed out to the front door of the chateau.

A cold night's breeze greeted her, and she was glad she'd worn her cosy Fair Isle jumper.

'I'll walk you back safely to the cottage,' Struan offered.

'No, I'm fine. It's a short walk.'

'I insist.'

He carried her bag and together they walked out into the snowy night.

Lucy took a deep breath. 'The air is so fresh here. I love it. And I love the quietude.' She stopped talking as they walked. They heard only the sound of the snow crunch beneath their feet.

They arrived at the cottage and Struan handed her the bag. 'You did look lovely in those dresses.'

She unlocked the front door, kicked the snow from her boots and stepped inside. Struan remained outside. He noticed her blush slightly.

'Thanks for everything, Struan, goodnight.'

He went to walk away and then said, 'While I'm here, could I have a look at your art portfolio?'

'Come in. You can take it with you.'

He followed her into the lounge. 'I'll light the fire for you.'

She flicked her desk lamp on. 'You can take this portfolio with you.'

'Are you sure you don't need it for your work?'

'No, I'm not using it.' She held up another portfolio. 'This is the one with the collection of artwork for the new book.'

He came over to her desk, having coaxed the fire into life. 'Can I have a look?'

She turned each page slowly. 'These are the illustrations I drew today. I add each finished piece of artwork into the portfolio. It helps me see it starting to look like a book.'

He pointed to one of the illustrations. 'Those bluebells look lovely.'

'Scottish bluebells are such pretty flowers. These are part of the new book, but you'll find similar bluebell designs in the other portfolio.'

'I like the snowdrops too.'

She turned to the next page.

'Ah, is this the squirrel you were telling me about?'

'It is. What do you think?'

'He's great, especially with all the leaves and acorns.'

She closed the new portfolio and handed him the other one.

'I'll take good care of it,' he said.

They stood together for a moment by the glow of the fire.

'Can I ask you something?' he began hesitantly.

She nodded.

'What convinced you to agree to take part in Bret's film?'

'Two things. The first was when Bret said it was a chance to be captured on film for all time. I liked the thought of that. The second was because of Marcia. She told me I'd make enough money to buy a cottage.'

His eyes showed hopefulness. 'Is that something you want to do? To buy a cottage here? You'd move away from the city?'

She hesitated. 'I've always been a city type, but lately I've found living there quite stressful, and the thought of being in a quiet little cottage away from the hustle and bustle appeals to me.'

'I'm glad.'

'Why?' she asked.

His stunning blue eyes gazed longingly at her. 'I think you know why,' he said softly.

Realising he'd said too much, he tapped the portfolio. 'I'll get this back to you soon.' He headed out of the lounge. 'Remember you've got the use of the whirlpool.'

'I'm going to take you up on that offer, just not tonight. I'm bone weary and emotionally exhausted.'

He stepped outside. 'Kissing and dancing with a handsome film star will do that to you.' His tone was teasing.

'Kissing and canoodling with someone else will do it even more.'

He smiled at her. 'Goodnight, Lucy.'

She closed the door and hurried through to the window to watch him walk away. She might have kissed Sanderson that night, but her heart yearned to belong to someone else.

Heckie brought milk and groceries to Lucy's cottage early the following morning.

She invited him into the kitchen for a cup of tea.

'I'm under strict instructions from Struan not to stay long as you're busy,' said Heckie.

'I won't tell if you don't.'

He grinned and sat down at the kitchen table.

She made tea and asked him about Struan. Heckie had worked for Struan's parents and had known him for many years. She found out a few things about Struan's past from him. . .

'When Struan lost his parents it was a terrible time. But Struan knew the success of the chateau now depended on him. He'd already worked with his parents in the business and managed the chateau when they went abroad on holiday, so he continued on, and we were all grateful to keep our jobs.'

'Has he ever had a serious girlfriend?'

'I've known Struan since he was a lad. He's never had lots of girlfriends, but any women he's been involved with have invariably caused him heartache. He's got a great head for business but no sense when it comes to romance.'

'I suppose they see him as a meal ticket.'

Heckie nodded. 'Brona and I, and some of the other staff, have long hoped that one day a nice young woman would arrive at the chateau. Someone he could settle down with.'

'Does Struan live in the chateau? Brona mentioned something about a lodge.'

'The lodge is his house.' Heckie pointed out the kitchen window. 'See those trees away over there? That's where he had it built five

73

years ago. He wanted somewhere private to live. It's a beauty. Very traditional. Old–fashioned some would call it. I helped install the kitchen. There's a proper stove, two butler–style sinks, an oak table and chairs in the centre. All the modern appliances, but chosen to fit in with traditional values. I fair love it.'

'It sounds idyllic.'

'It is — and with you being a floral illustrator, you'd appreciate the garden. It's got all the flowers you could wish for. Tea roses, a chamomile lawn, lots of flowers to encourage bees and butterflies. Struan loves gardening. It's his hobby, not that he gets time for it.'

'I'd love to see it.'

'It'll be covered in snow, but you should ask him to show you the lodge.'

'I may give him a subtle hint.'

'Nah, just ask him outright,' Heckie advised her.

'Better to be straightforward,' she agreed.

'In the city, people tend to keep their noses out of other folks business. But here we're apt to interfere and nosey. So I'll ask. . . are you happy living in the city? Have you any plans to settle down? Or is your book career the centre of your world?'

'The books and my work are my main priority. But I can't just live in a work bubble. Somewhere along the line I've skewed my priorities to focus on little else.' She glanced around. 'However, being here in the cottage, away from everything, makes me long for a life like this rather than living in a flat in the city.'

'With your type of career, you could work almost anywhere.'

Lucy nodded. 'That's what Struan said.'

A twinkle flashed in Heckie's eyes. 'And what about Struan? Could you picture having a man like him in your life?'

She could. A rose blush swept across her features. No need to tell Heckie how she felt about Struan.

Heckie drank down the remainder of his tea and stood up. 'I'll let you get on now, Lucy. And if you'd like a smidgen of advice from an old boy like me, don't let the love of a lifetime slip past you for the sake of work, or you'll have nothing to look back on except a string of deadlines.'

She nodded up at him.

'I'd better get back to the chateau. Sanderson's doing the staircase stunt today. They didn't have time for it last night, so the

74

director asked me to polish the balustrades again.' He sounded proud as he said, 'I put a layer of beeswax on them. Smooth as butter. Sanderson will slide down easily.' He smiled at her. 'I'll see myself out.'

When Heckie left, the quietude hit her. She was alone again while the world outside swirled around her.

Tempted as she was to pop up to the chateau to watch Sanderson's slide stunt, she instead went through to her desk, set up a fresh sheet of layout paper and put it over her pencil drawings of delphiniums, Queen Anne's lace plant, lavender and bumblebees on her artist light box. Then she picked up her finest nib black ink pen and began drawing the finished artwork of the flowers and bees.

The stunt fight coordinator put Sanderson through his paces on the staircase, practising the daring slide down the balustrade and landing on the safety mats at the bottom.

Sanderson wore tight–fitting faux suede trousers that laced up the front, and a flamboyant white shirt open almost to the waist.

'I feel like a modern–day swashbuckler in this outfit,' Sanderson said to Bret, playfully swinging an invisible cutlass through the air.

'Remember,' Bret told him, 'for this scene, speed is everything. We need more buckle than swash.'

Sanderson nodded then said, 'Charmaine's been hounding me. She wants to punch me when I land instead of kissing me.'

Bret gave Sanderson's shoulder a reassuring pat. 'I'll talk to her.'

Numerous guests who had volunteered to be part of the background milled about, ready to play their part. Excited faces all round.

As requested by Bret, Heckie entwined silver tinsel under the balustrades to add a dash of festive sparkle.

Struan, smartly dressed in a dark suit, whispered to Heckie. 'Did you drop off the groceries to Lucy?'

'I did, and when I left she was about to get on with her illustrations. I was telling her about your garden at the lodge. She seemed interested. Maybe you should invite her over for a look?'

'You weren't supposed to distract her, Heckie.'

'I only mentioned it while unpacking the milk and bread.' He frowned at Struan. 'Are you okay this morning? You seem awfy wound up.'

Struan ran an agitated hand through his hair, pushing back the strands that refused to be tamed. 'I've been up half the night looking through Lucy's art portfolio. The night got away from me. One minute I was admiring the hollyhocks, the next the dawn was rising. I drank a pot of strong coffee, you know how Brona makes it, thick as tar. My insides are jumping. I don't know whether it's the lack of sleep, the potent coffee or watching Sanderson sliding down that ruddy staircase like a well–oiled fly.'

Heckie threw in another option. 'Or Lucy?'

'What about Lucy?'

Heckie gave him a knowing wink. 'Lucy could cause many a man to be distracted.'

'Where is Lucy?' Bret said, joining them. 'Isn't she here to watch the stunt?'

'She's busy working on her new designs in the cottage,' said Struan. 'She has a tight deadline and needs to catch up for lost time.'

Sanderson sauntered over. 'You work Lucy too hard, Struan. Bret and I were talking about her last night. Behind her smiles, she seems stressed.'

Struan sounded exasperated. 'That's because she's behind with her deadline. Now she needs to work harder.'

Bret smiled at Struan. 'Be careful. I may steal Lucy and whisk her away to a better life in L.A.'

Struan smiled back, though it was more like a grimace. 'If you try that, I'd fight you for her, and trust me, my ire would contain more swash than buckle.'

Bret laughed and threw his arm around Struan's shoulders. 'Take it easy, bud. Remember, guys like us can never own a Lucy.'

'Why not?' asked Struan.

'We could never be that lucky.'

Marcia thrust the script schedule under Bret's nose. 'The studio phoned.'

'Don't these guys ever sleep?' said Sanderson.

'They're accommodating us, working our time zone,' Marcia reminded him.

'What do they need?' Bret asked her.

'They want assurances the staircase stunt will be in today's dailies.'

'We're about to shoot it now,' said Bret.

Marcia marched off, pressing speed dial on her phone.

'Okay, folks,' Bret shouted. 'Everyone in position. Let's roll. . . '

'Do you want a wee sprinkling of chives on your mashed tatties?' Donnan asked. He'd arrived to deliver her lunch.

'Yes, please.' She cleared a space on the kitchen table and sat down while Donnan busied himself around her.

'How are you getting on with your flower drawings today?'

She sounded delighted. 'Really well. I've got a lot done. I even finished the pansies, lily of the valley and heliotrope.'

'Good on you. I wouldn't know one flower from the next, except for roses. I buy bunches of them for my girlfriend. She loves roses.'

'That's very romantic of you, Donnan.'

He looked guilty. 'I'm always doing something wrong, but if I buy her roses all is usually forgiven.'

Lucy smiled at him. 'Whatever the reason, I'm sure she appreciates them.'

He set up a side plate. 'I brought you a slice of apple pie. If you don't want it for lunch, wrap it up and put it in the fridge for later.'

'You're spoiling me.'

He grinned and then relayed some gossip.

'I overheard Bret and Struan talking about you.'

'What did they say?' she asked him.

'You never heard this from me. . .' Donnan confided. 'Bret jokingly threatened to steal you away to Hollywood. Then Struan said he'd fight Bret for you. It was all guy talk if you know what I mean. Posturing, poking fun, but the underlying rivalry was there. Totally palpable.'

Lucy's eyes widened. 'Struan said he'd fight for me?'

'Uh–huh.' Donnan closed the hamper he'd brought to bring her food. 'Sorry lunch was late again, but there are carrots today to go with your cabbage.'

'Another rumpus at the chateau?' she said lightly.

'Didn't you hear the helicopter landing and taking off again?'

'I did. I assumed it was guests arriving at the chateau.'

Donnan shook his head. 'No, they were flying Sanderson away for X–rays. He said his injuries were no more than bruises and a pulled muscle in his leg, but Bret insisted for insurance purposes.'

'Whatever happened? Was this for the staircase stunt?'

77

'It was. The first time he slid down the balustrade fast and landed perfectly. But Charmaine spoiled the shot by trying to punch him. So he had to do it again, and this time he was wary of her fist at the end of the stairs and held back a bit. He slid down but it wasn't as spectacular. The director made him do it a third time. Tempers were ragged. Sanderson was so defiant that he slid down even faster and overshot at the bottom. He skited right past Charmaine, slid along the foyer floor and nearly went as far as the craft shop.'

'Why do I keep missing the memorable stuff?' she huffed. 'I guess they'll have to postpone the stunt until another day.'

'No. Bret's schedule is tight. They're filming the scene again later today.'

'Will Sanderson be back on time?'

'It's not Sanderson who is doing the stunt now — it's Struan.'

She almost shouted. 'Struan?'

'They're stitching him into Sanderson's trousers as we speak.'

'Stitching him in?'

'The trousers were skin tight on Sanderson. When he landed, the lace ups on the front burst at the seams. If he hadn't been wearing boxers, everyone would've seen his winkie. So they're making sure Struan doesn't come undone.'

Lucy felt the colour drain from her face.

'Are you okay?'

'I'm worried Struan will hurt himself.'

Donnan brushed this notion aside. 'Nonsense. Struan's slid down that balustrade since he was a boy. Sometimes he still does if we've had a wild party. He definitely did it last New Year — so did Heckie and some of the others. It's a skoosh.'

'Have you ever done it?'

'Och aye, plenty of times.'

Lucy was anxious. 'I don't think I can settle and concentrate on my artwork until I know Struan's okay. Maybe I should come and help?'

'No, no that's a bad idea. You could distract him, and that's the last thing he needs.'

'You're right,' she said, disappointed.

Donnan gave her a mischievous grin. 'But you could come and watch if you wore a disguise.'

'What type of disguise?'

He pointed to her food. 'You get that down you. I'll run up to the chateau and fetch you a set of chef whites. Pretend you're one of the catering staff. Merge with the melee.'

Giving her no time to think or object, Donnan raced away to set their madcap scheme in motion.

'Pull your hat down and walk beside me,' Donnan instructed Lucy as they headed into the chateau. She wore a loose–fitting chef's uniform and a worried expression.

'The staff will recognise me,' she whispered.

'Of course they will, but it's not them you're hiding from, it's Struan. Now buck up and look like you know what you're doing.'

What was she doing? She'd let herself be persuaded to do this. In the cottage it seemed like a fine idea, but under the glare of the film crew's lights, she felt exposed and vulnerable.

'There's Struan,' said Donnan. 'Keep your head down.' He grabbed a tray of petits fours. 'Hold this and look down as we walk past Struan.'

Lucy did exactly as Donnan suggested, but nothing prepared her for the effect Struan had on her senses when she saw his fit physique in the flamboyant shirt. It was undone to the waist and exposed the smooth chest she'd been so close to recently. Then there was the tight–fitting, faux suede trousers that emphasised his long, lean–muscled thighs and other parts of his physique. Jeez, those trousers were a cause for celebration and consternation. A wardrobe assistant checked the stitching on the lace up thongs holding in his manliness. That he let her do this disturbed Lucy, even though it was totally professional.

'Your petits fours are rattling, Lucy. Hold your nerve, lass.' Donnan's attempt at a pep talk worked. She tried to calm down.

'What's Heckie doing?' she asked Donnan.

'Giving the balustrade a quick buff. I think they're getting ready to film now. We'll stand over beside the boutique to watch.'

Marcia waylaid them as they walked across the foyer, carefully stepping around the safety landing mats.

Marcia's eyes looked at the petits fours. 'Are those marzipan?'

Lucy nodded, keeping her head down, and offered the tray up to Marcia who selected two without glancing at her and walked over to join Bret.

CHAPTER NINE

Romance and Kisses

'What are you up to, Lucy?' Brona said, seeing her standing outside the boutique with Donnan.

'She's spying on Struan,' he answered for her.

'I am not,' Lucy stated firmly, but kept her voice down.

Donnan iced her with a look.

'Okay,' Lucy admitted. 'I'm sort of spying on Struan.'

Brona tried not to laugh.

'She didn't want to upset his concentration,' Donnan explained. 'And she didn't want to miss the spectacle either.'

Heckie went by, blinked twice and gave the strange chef a quizzical look. When he saw Brona stifling a grin, he realised it was Lucy and came hurrying over.

'What's going on?' Heckie said, smiling.

Donnan explained.

'Don't worry, Lucy,' Heckie assured her. 'During the practice runs, Struan was fine and landed safely on the mats every time. We just have to hope he can do it in those costume trousers, but I've buffed the balustrades so the fabric doesn't cause friction.'

'Everyone to their places,' a crew member announced. Several cameras were set to film it from all angles.

Lucy glanced over at Struan. He looked like a Hollywood action star, so tall and handsome. His hair had been tamed with a lavish amount of gel and hairspray, and makeup applied to make him appear even more like Sanderson.

'At a distance Struan looks quite like Sanderson,' Brona said to Lucy.

'He does.'

Donnan added, 'Bret said that because it's a fast–action stunt, Struan will pass for the actor because no one will have time to see him. He'll whiz down the stairs, and then Charmaine will run into his arms and kiss him.'

'Struan's going to kiss Charmaine?'

'Calm down, Lucy,' said Brona. 'It's just acting.'

Lucy tried to look calm when inside her stomach knotted.

Struan kept looking around moments before the scene began.

'What's Struan looking for?' asked Lucy.

Brona nudged her. 'You, silly.'

This made Lucy feel slightly better.

'Everyone ready,' Bret shouted, 'and. . . action!'

Struan ran up the stairs, while Charmaine struggled to escape from the clutches of the villain. Wriggling free, she called for help to Struan. He turned, jumped astride the balustrade and came sliding down at speed.

Lucy's heart squeezed seeing how magnificent he was, and the way he landed was worthy of a gymnast. But as he grasped hold of Charmaine and turned away from the camera so it picked up his back view, and kissed her, Lucy let out a horrible gasp. The sound resonated in the foyer, but the cameras kept rolling.

'Cut!' Bret shouted finally, looking around to see who had yelled out.

'Is it ruined?' Struan asked Bret. 'Will I have to do it again?'

Bret checked the playback while listening to Struan. The director seemed more concerned with the visual aspects, not the sound.

'This looks amazing,' Bret shouted, punching the air. 'We got the money shot. Struan — you nailed it, buddy.' He gave Struan a shoulder hug. 'Don't worry about the weird sound. I'll erase it in the editing suite.'

Struan was relieved he didn't have to do it again, though Charmaine was quite willing to kiss him repeatedly.

Struan looked around again, amid the crowd cheering and people happy with their own little performances as part of the background.

Lucy stared at Struan. His gaze swept past her, then he sensed her watching. 'Lucy?' he mouthed to her.

She nodded.

He ran over and laughed when she explained why she was dressed as a chef.

'I kept hoping you'd be here,' said Struan, taking a tissue to wipe Charmaine's lipstick from his mouth. 'I was looking for you. I never expected you to be in disguise.'

'Blame me,' said Donnan.

Struan laughed and pointed at all of them. 'You were all in on it, but I'm grateful.'

'You looked like a film star,' Brona told him.

Heckie nodded. 'And your breeks didn't burst.'

Struan squirmed as if the outfit wasn't to his taste.

'I think we'll have to get back to the kitchens,' said Brona, tugging at Donnan and Heckie, a less than subtle hint to leave Struan and Lucy alone.

Struan gently lifted Lucy's hat off and her hair came tumbling down. He put the hat and tray aside. 'Look at us, we must be crazy.'

'Something to look back on when all this is over.'

He leaned down and gazed at her. 'Does it have to be over?'

'I don't know.'

'At least that's sort of a hopeful answer,' he said as lively party music started to play in the background, coming from one of the function rooms. 'Bret's having a late lunch party. We're invited.'

'I'm not exactly dressed for it.'

'I could walk you back to the cottage to change.'

She nodded, and they headed outside while the party got underway.

The air was cold and yet neither of them really noticed it. They were too wrapped up in each other, chatting about the day's events — her artwork and his daring stunt.

'Bret wants us to film a couple of early morning shots, if you're up for it,' he told her. 'He wants you to wear the silver dress. He says it'll be the last scenes he'll need before they leave.'

'What about the daring leap Sanderson was going to do off the roof of the chateau?' she asked. 'Will Bret have to cut that out altogether?'

Struan shrugged, causing her heart to ache just looking at his manly build in the low–cut shirt. 'Sanderson's flying back later.'

'I'm relieved he's okay.'

'Nothing more than bruises, though he's been advised not to dance or do anything that could hurt his strained muscles. So the rooftop stunt isn't an option, unless someone else does it.'

'Oh no, Struan. You shouldn't. It's too dangerous.'

'Bret says if I do it, they'll be able to finish the film on schedule. A lot of people's livelihoods depend on it. We both know how that works.'

Lucy nodded, thinking how her editor was relying on her.

They went inside the cottage and Lucy got changed in the bedroom. She put on a pair of black trousers and a lovely blue top.

Struan was in the lounge having a look at her latest artwork. 'I love the heliotrope and Queen Anne's lace.'

'You really do know your flowers.'

'I've had a browse through your portfolio, but because of what happened I haven't had time to select anything. Can I have another day or two to look through it?'

'Of course. Take your time.'

They headed back up to the chateau. It gave a welcome glow in the late afternoon light. Although Lucy hadn't been there long, it gave her a warm feeling, a sense of being home.

'I'll miss this,' she said, letting her thoughts slip out.

'Me too,' he murmured.

She stopped and frowned at him. 'But you're not leaving. You're not going home to the city.'

He paused and stood beside her. He motioned to everything around them, and included them. 'I'll miss you, us, our time here. Some of it feels like a scene from Bret's film. I'm just hoping for a happy ending.'

'What would that ending look like to you?'

'Like this, more afternoons like this, and days together with Lucy Fantastic.'

She laughed at him — and then gazed up at the roof. 'It's quite high.'

'I'd land safely on an airbag.'

He bit his lip and she saw how much he wanted to do this.

She went to walk on, but he pulled her to him. 'Can I do something before we go in?'

She looked up at him. 'What's that?'

He kissed her, long and hard and then with tenderness and passion.

He whispered to her. 'I didn't feel comfortable kissing Charmaine. I just want you to know.'

She smiled warmly.

Marcia saw them and hurried over. 'Bret needs that rooftop stunt. Guys in the crew are willing to do it, but none of them look like Sanderson. Will you do it, Struan?'

He glanced at Lucy. She nodded reluctantly. 'Okay, Marcia, I'll do it.'

'We'll set it up right now. Keep those clothes on.' She hurried to tell Bret.

Lucy pulled up the collar of her warm jacket and stood in the front garden of the chateau gazing up at Struan standing on the rooftop balcony. Below, an airbag had been inflated and the stunt coordinator had instructed Struan on the best way to land.

'I can't believe I didn't talk him out of this,' Lucy said to Brona.

'Struan's a strong, strapping man, Lucy. He can do it.'

A crowd had gathered to watch. Lucy heard their chatter, then it all faded as every part of her focussed on Struan. She was sure, just before he took the daring leap, he'd looked down at her, and only her.

And then he jumped.

Every available film camera captured the scene. Bret assured him he'd only have to do it once. A one–shot deal.

Lucy held her breath, watching him fall.

He landed safely on the airbag and a rousing cheer went up. Something else Bret would have to erase from the final edits.

The crew helped Struan down from the bag. He waved at Lucy and ran over to her, wrapping her in a hug.

'Never, ever do anything like that again, okay?' she said.

He smiled broadly. 'Okay.'

A helicopter arrived and dropped off Sanderson. 'Am I late for the party?'

As the crew packed away the airbag, the crowd filtered back into the chateau, and as Sanderson was welcomed by Bret and Charmaine, all was right with the world.

Lucy breathed in the moment, committing it to memory, and walked back inside with Struan.

'Someone is going to have to cut you out of those pants,' Sanderson said to Struan.

Sanderson languished on a chair beside the Christmas tree being pampered. He had his wrist strapped up, but apart from that, no one would've guessed he'd been through the wringer.

'Do you enjoy wearing costumes like this?' Struan asked him.

'Sure. It's fun.'

'I'm going to my room to shower and change,' Struan told Lucy. She walked with him to the foyer.

'I'll see you later,' she said.

'Aren't you staying for the party?'

'I've changed my mind, but I'll be back later.'

Lucy walked back to the cottage, planning to get on with her drawings.

The fire still had some heat in it. She piled on more logs and settled down at her desk.

A floral basket design needed finished.

While Lucy drew the wings of a butterfly, and embellished a design with pretty daisies, an email arrived from her editor asking if she'd settled in and was making progress with the book.

Lucy typed a reply telling her that she was sitting at her desk working on the illustrations, all cosy in the cottage beside a log fire with snow falling gently outside the window. It sounded idyllic, and it was. She attached images of her recent finished artwork and sent the email.

A reply popped up a short while later from her editor. She loved the new designs and was delighted that Lucy was happy in the cottage.

Lucy continued working for the next hour or so until she needed to take a break. She got up and stretched, went over to the window and peered out at the snow which was now falling heavier. Not quite a blizzard, but with the potential to cover the landscape with a fresh layer of sparkling white flakes.

She made a cup of tea and sat beside the fire, glazing at the flickering flames, relishing the quietude, thinking of Struan and the others. Then she thought about her editor and Ella, and her flat in the city. Two sides of the same coin. She felt as if she was on the tipping point of leaving one part of her life behind in exchange for something shiny and new. Was it the right thing to do? Was it? Would she feel differently if she was at home? Ella would have the Christmas tree up and the flat would be abuzz with festive songs and singing. Ella was always so cheerful and full of life. Was that such a bad thing? Only if you were an artist who preferred a quieter life.

Lucy cupped her tea and mulled over her future. The way Struan looked at her, she knew he wanted a relationship. But would this be like a holiday romance? It was certainly a romantic setting. She could hardly picture anything else so Christmassy and cosy.

When Lucy woke up, it was almost midnight. She'd fallen asleep on the sofa.

The fire smouldered in the hearth, but the lounge had retained the warmth. She got up and went through to the kitchen and made a cup of tea. Feeling rested, but unsettled, she thought about doing some more artwork, but then reconsidered. She'd end up working into the night and then be tired the next day when she'd agreed to take part in filming. No, she wouldn't do any more work. She didn't want to go to bed either, so she decided this was the ideal evening to take Struan up on his offer of using the whirlpool at midnight.

The night porter showed Lucy where the fitness suite was and left her to enjoy the whirlpool, having assured her no one would disturb her.

It was situated at the back of the chateau with an expanse of windows giving a view of the rear garden. It has stopped snowing, and the frozen garden shimmered in the lights from the hotel.

Lucy changed out of her clothes, pinned her hair up in a butterfly clasp and wrapped herself in a large, white towel. She padded through to the whirlpool. Soft overhead spotlights created a lovely atmosphere and the warm, bubbling water looked inviting.

She hadn't brought any type of swimwear with her, but having the private use of the facility, she felt free to slip the towel off and step into the warm water. She relaxed back. It was sheer luxury. The tension in her shoulders eased and she was glad she'd decided to do this rather than work.

Relaxing in the whirlpool, she had a view of the snowy garden. Yes, she thought, this was the life.

She wasn't sure how much time had passed before she heard a tentative knock on the fitness suite door.

'Lucy? Are you in there? Are you decent?'

Her heart jumped. 'Struan?'

'Yes, I don't want to disturb you.'

'You can come in if you don't peek. I'm wearing nothing but bubbles.'

Struan clicked the door open and ventured in, trying to look anywhere except at Lucy. 'I just wanted to make sure you were okay. You sort of disappeared and no one had heard from you. You didn't even phone up to the chateau to order dinner.'

'I was on a creative roll with my work and kept going. Then I fell asleep.'

'Splendid. I hope you got a lot done.'

'I did. I emailed some of the finished designs to my editor and she's delighted.'

'The plan's working then? Keeping you hunkered in the cottage.'

'It is. I've caught up with my deadline.'

'Brilliant. Remember about the filming tomorrow morning. Do you want an early morning alarm call?'

She thought about it. 'Under the circumstances, I'm going to say yes.'

'I'll mark that into the log at reception.'

'How is Sanderson?'

'Fine. We put him in the whirlpool earlier this evening to ease his bruises. We had to haul him out. He'd have stayed in there for hours. He loved it. Bret took advantage of the situation and filmed him in it with Charmaine.'

There was an awkward silence.

'I suppose I should leave you to relax, Lucy.'

'I won't be much longer. I'll get dried off, dressed and walk back to the cottage.'

'Did you bring a warm jacket? The contrast of being in the heat and then outside in the freezing air could give you a chill.'

'I brought warm clothing,' she assured him.

'Fine. I'm heading to the lodge to get some sleep.'

'I'll see you in the morning, Struan.'

'Yes. The night porter will help with anything else you need.'

Struan looked over at her momentarily before leaving.

'No peeking.'

'I wasn't, Lucy. I, eh. . . goodnight.' He hurried out and probably heard her laughing.

CHAPTER TEN

Christmas Cake Ceilidh

A fist pounded on the door of Lucy's cottage.

She jerked awake, then realised she'd slept in. She jumped out of bed wearing her cosy jim–jams, stuck her feet into fluffy slippers and ran through to open the door.

'You've slept through your alarm you,' said Struan. 'Hurry up, Lucy, we're going to be late.'

He stepped inside wearing an expensive jacket over his suit.

Lucy ran through to the bedroom, threw off her pyjamas and ransacked her wardrobe for something warm but stylish to wear. Her grey trousers and a jumper came to hand. These would do.

'Remember to put the silver dress on,' Struan called through to her.

She threw the trousers and jumper aside. 'Yes, of course,' she said, trailing the silver dress off the hanger and putting it on.

He heard manic rumbling noises from the bedroom. 'Are you all right in there?'

'The straps of the dress are twisted. I can't reach round the back to sort them.'

'I'm coming in, Lucy.'

Struan entered and helped straighten the thin straps. The dress dipped down low on the back, and it was obvious she wore nothing underneath the top half. He felt his heart thunder in his chest and hoped she couldn't sense the effect her smooth skin and sexy figure had on him.

He started to search through her belongings for her evening shoes and boots while she brushed her hair and applied some makeup.

She turned to face him. 'How's my hair? Does it look like I've been wrestling monkeys in my sleep?'

'No, you've tamed it, but we need to run. Bret wants to film early morning shots while it's not snowing.'

He thrust her shoes in his jacket pockets and hustled her out of the bedroom. Her jacket was hanging in the hallway. She put it on quickly along with her boots.

Struan stepped out into the snow. Lucy followed him, trying to hold up the hem of her long dress from being ruined in the snow. It was slowing her down, slowing them down.

Struan kept waiting for her to catch up, then finally as she almost toppled, he lifted her up and threw her over his shoulder.

'We're making a habit of this,' she said, giggling.

'Stop making me laugh, Lucy.' But he couldn't help himself.

The crew were all set ready for filming.

Bret cheered as Struan ran up to him with Lucy, keeping her over his shoulder while they spoke.

'Her dress was trailing in the snow,' Struan explained, making no mention of her tardiness.

'I think we'll include this. Don't put her down Struan.' Bret turned his face at an awkward angle and leaned down to talk to Lucy. 'Morning, Lucy. Can you hold that position?'

'Yes.'

'Great. Both of you keep your jackets on.' Bret took the shoes from Struan's pockets. 'But we'll change her boots for the shoes.'

Wardrobe assistants pulled Lucy's boots off and slipped the shoes on. Someone dabbed her nose with powder.

'We're going to take advantage of the snowscape,' said Bret. 'Struan, I want you to walk over there, then when I signal, we'll film you running with Lucy across the snow to the chateau.'

Struan carried Lucy while the cameras were set to film them.

'This shouldn't take long,' Struan said to her. 'Are you okay?'

'Oh yes. Never better.'

Bret gave the signal and Struan ran with her. She tried not to laugh.

'Cut,' shouted Bret.

Struan went to put Lucy down then realised he couldn't let her stand in the snow in her evening shoes. He ended up placing his winter jacket down for her to stand on.

'We'll do another take, this time without your jackets,' said Bret.

Lucy shrugged her jacket off and tried not to gasp when the cold hit her.

Struan lifted her up immediately and carried her in his arms to their starting position. She had her arm around his shoulder and saw the breath pour from his sensual lips as he spoke.

'I'll take you back for a hot breakfast as soon as Bret's happy with the scene.'

'Thank you, Struan.' She was near his face, and could see his gorgeous blue eyes so clear and bright in the morning light.

Struan then lifted her over his shoulder and ran again across the snow. A wonderful feeling surged through him. This was one of those moments when everything was right — carrying Lucy in her beautiful silver dress, unrestricted by their jackets, the touch of her skin and the shimmering fabric, a sense of excitement, running fast with the winter light making everything sparkle.

'Cut,' Bret shouted, sounding pleased. He immediately checked the playback. 'Yes, this is amazing. A few shots of the two of you with the chateau in the background and a couple of close–ups, then we're done.'

Seeing Lucy on her own made Bret consider an extra shot. 'Lucy, how do you feel about running in the snow towards Struan? You jump up and wrap your arms around his neck. He catches you, swings you around in his arms and kisses you. Could you do that?'

Lucy nodded.

These shots were taken swiftly, and then Lucy was wrapped in her jacket and boots put back on.

While Bret and the crew continued filming with Sanderson and Charmaine, Struan took Lucy to the cottage to change out of her dress and into warm clothes.

'That was quite an experience,' she called to him from the bedroom.

'I wonder if Bret will use it in the film?'

She walked through to the lounge, dressed in trousers, a cosy jumper and cardigan. 'Bret seemed pleased with the shots, though I guess we'll have to wait until the film is released.'

'It's scheduled for November next year. That's when the premiere is in Hollywood, followed by one in London.'

Struan's phone rang. It was a message from Brona. He relayed the call the Lucy. 'There's chaos at the chateau. A bit of filming fiasco. I have to go. I'll have someone bring breakfast down to you.'

Struan left Lucy at the cottage. She sat at her desk and began drawing, all the while thinking about Struan and the way he made her feel great when she was in his arms.

By mid–day the blue winter sky had dimmed to a stormy grey, and it started snowing.

Lucy buttoned up her cardigan and opened the patio doors, making sure she had a key to get back in if they closed behind her. She stepped out and watched the large flakes of snow swirl across the sky, becoming heavier. The wind buffeted the cottage and she was forced to go back in.

She peered out the window at the blizzard, feeling safe and cosy in the cottage.

Struan phoned Lucy in the late afternoon. 'Bret and the crew are getting ready to leave.'

'I'll come up to wish them well.'

'Wrap up, it's blustery.'

'I will.'

Lucy put on her jacket and wore a woolly hat she'd knitted. She trudged through the snow, feeling the icy flakes against her cheeks. By the time she arrived at the chateau, brushing the snow from her clothes, her cheeks were rosy.

Bret, Sanderson, Charmaine and the others were gathered in the foyer. A helicopter had landed and was ready to whisk the stars away. Others prepared to drive, despite the blustery conditions.

Bret gave Lucy a hug. 'This is not goodbye forever. We expect to see you at the premieres. No excuses accepted.'

'Okay, Bret. I'll be there. And I'll send out the press release and pics to the media after you've gone,' she promised.

'Thanks, Lucy.'

Bret then hugged Struan. 'I expect to see you too.'

Struan nodded.

'The helicopter is ready to leave,' a crew member called to Sanderson and Charmaine.

On his way out, Sanderson kissed Lucy Fantastic, and thanked Struan for making them all feel so welcome.

Charmaine hurried on, then turned and waved from a distance.

As the actors and crew headed to the helicopter and got into the vehicles, Marcia hurried over to Lucy and handed her a business card.

'This has my private phone number and email contacts. When things are settled, I'm throwing a party in Los Angeles in the summer — friends only. I'll send you an invitation and tickets for the flight.'

Lucy took the card, but wondered if she'd heard right? Where in all of this had she become friends with Marcia?

Marcia smiled at Lucy and gave her a hug. 'You've been great. You've gone along with everything we asked of you. Some people are total asses.' She smiled again. 'Keep in contact. I'll let you know I arrive safe. I don't let trusted friendships drift. And I totally expect a copy of your new book when it comes out, signed of course.'

And so Lucy had made a new friend whether she wanted it or not. But she decided that Marcia probably had hidden depths of warmth. Maybe.

Struan and Lucy stood together with the chateau staff and waved everyone off. 'I'm sure we'll see them again,' he said.

'I'm certain we will,' Lucy agreed.

Then it was time to get everything ready for the ceilidh.

'Are you coming to the ceilidh tonight?' Struan asked Lucy.

'Yes, I'd like that.'

'Great,' he said and hurried off to organise the function room and catering with Heckie and Donnan.

Lucy was left chatting to Brona.

Brona smiled. 'You and Marcia, pals forever, eh?'

'Did I miss something?'

Brona shrugged. 'A friend in Hollywood is no bad thing.'

'What should I wear for the ceilidh? Would a skirt and a white blouse be suitable?'

'Oh, yes, but wear shoes you can dance in,' said Brona.

'I've got a pair of black pumps that would do.'

Brona glanced at the craft shop. 'We've got tartan sashes if you'd like one of those to wear with your blouse.'

Lucy was interested and went into the shop with Brona to pick one up. She chose a lovely tartan sash, and as she went to pay for it at the craft shop counter, she noticed her colouring books on display.

'Your books arrived this morning,' said Brona. 'They look wonderful.'

The craft shop assistant wrapped Lucy's sash and said that she liked Lucy's books too.

While she was in, Lucy eyed the gorgeous selection of yarns and had a notion to knit something. It always helped her to relax. So she bought several balls of yarn and knitting needles. Brona said she would bring her knitting patterns for a bobble hat and scarf set the following day.

While Lucy walked back to the cottage with a bag filled with yarn and the tartan sash, Brona went behind the reception desk and wrote something in the staff register.

Brona saw Struan go by.

'Struan,' Brona called to him. 'I've pencilled in my spring holiday fortnight dates.'

Struan smiled happily. 'Going on holiday down the coast again this year to the seaside?' He seemed sure she would. She'd done this for years rather than go abroad.

'No, I'm going abroad to get some sunshine.'

He was taken aback. 'Abroad, Brona?'

'Yes, I've never ventured far, but I think it's time I did. I'm going to California. I've got a friend there. She's invited me to stay with her.'

'I'm delighted for you. Consider the dates yours.'

As Struan continued on to the function room to organise the ceilidh, Brona sent a text message to Charmaine confirming she'd be visiting her soon.

The Christmas cake for the ceilidh sat in pride of place on the buffet table that was set up opposite the small stage area where a band were playing lively music.

Lucy walked in, unsure whether she knew any of the dances. It had been ages since she'd been to a ceilidh with Ella. She wore her black pumps, having changed out of her boots in the cloakroom.

Giving her no time to ponder, Struan welcomed her to the party, sweeping her into a fast–swirling reel.

Lucy was soon so caught up in the energy and merriment that she didn't worry about not knowing all the steps. Some guests were well acquainted with the dances, while others were in a similar position to

Lucy, or had no idea what to do, but joined in the fun anyway. Everyone was made welcome.

Struan wore his kilt. Donnan was right. Struan suited it. He had great legs for a kilt, worn with cream wool hose and classic brogues. His white shirt and black waistcoat emphasised the width of his shoulders and lean, fit physique. He twirled her around the dance floor, and she didn't want to ask if he'd gone commando.

The large Christmas cake was cut by one of the chefs, and pieces given to the party guests.

'This is delicious,' Lucy said to Struan. 'Is there whisky in this fruit cake?'

Donnan overheard and answered for him. 'Whisky and some of the fruit is soaked in brandy. We also add a strong brew of tea.' Donnan walked on, serving other guests.

Lucy and Struan sat down together to enjoy their cake while the dancing continued.

'I'm having so much fun,' she said to him, and tucked into her cake.

'I've been looking through your portfolio. I've seen several floral pieces I'd like.'

'Do you want to show me?'

'The portfolio is at my lodge. Perhaps when we've exhausted ourselves dancing, you'd like to come back with me? I'll ply you with tea and another slice of our Christmas cake.'

Lucy nodded, and then they both got up and joined in a fast–moving reel.

The night air made Lucy shiver. Snow fluttered around them. She wore her boots and pulled the hood of her jacket up. Struan wore a hooded jacket too. He'd changed out of his kilt into casual but expensive black cords and cream knit jumper. He walked close beside her, making sure she didn't take a tumble.

'The lodge isn't far.' Struan pointed to the trees nearby.

Lucy saw the lodge ahead of them, tucked into a sheltered niche. The lodge was bigger than she'd imagined, at least twice the size of the cottage with a large garden. The lodge sat firmly in the centre.

Struan led the way to the front door and flicked the lights on as they stepped inside.

'Make yourself at home, Lucy. I'll get the fire lit.'

She walked through the lounge that had a wall of glass along one side overlooking the garden. Everything from the polished wood floors to the white–painted walls appealed to her sense of design. It was so classy. Manly yet homely. The sofa was cream with a vintage print, as were the cushions and occasional rugs. The most colourful rug in warm hues was in front of the fire. Struan knelt down on it and lit the fire. He piled on the logs. She could smell the fresh pine.

'Wow! This is lovely.'

She sensed he was nervous, hoping she liked it, so when she complimented it, he relaxed.

'The kitchen's through here.'

She followed him into one of the best kitchens she'd been in. Heckie's description was correct. It had all the modern appliances and yet the stove, dresser, tables and chairs had a vintage quality. Totally her taste.

Copper pans and other utensils hung on the walls, gleaming under the kitchen lights. Nothing looked worn, and she supposed he didn't cook here often. Why would he when the chateau could provide all his meals?

'I eat at the chateau mainly,' he said, as if reading her thoughts. 'But I can cook, although gardening is more my thing.'

She walked over to the window, again a large expanse of glass gave a view of the garden. The lodge was so airy and yet warm and welcoming.

She took her jacket off and put it on the back of a kitchen chair. The lodge didn't feel cold at all. She wore a cardigan over her blouse. She'd folded up the tartan sash and tucked it in her jacket pocket.

She watched Struan prepare tea, and there was a Christmas cake, uncut, on the table. He put plates down on a counter beside the dresser, and cut two wedges of cake while the old–fashioned kettle boiled.

She continued to watch him thoughtfully. . .

Here was the man from the chateau, away from his usual environment, and she could see the man who owned this lovely lodge. This was Struan, a successful hotel owner whose home was a spacious lodge, steeped in traditional decor. A man who loved to garden as a hobby. The garden looked like a fairytale, every plant and tree iced with snow crystals. The little pond where flowers no doubt thrived around the edges in summer was frozen. . .

'Here we are,' he said, serving up the tea and cake on a tray. 'We'll take it through to the lounge.'

He led the way, put the tray down on a coffee table, and they sat cosily in front of the fire having tea, cake and discussing Lucy's artwork.

'I like these Veronica blue flowers, and the snowdrops, bluebells and tea roses are definite choices.'

He'd bookmarked the pages of the portfolio with strips of paper.

She mentally noted the ones he wanted.

'The heliotrope you were illustrating is something I'd like too. I'd like them all, but we'll start with these.'

'I'll draw more heliotrope for you.'

'I also viewed the art on your website.' He pointed to the white walls in the lounge. 'These need paintings to give a dash of colour to the decor. What do you think? Large watercolours or acrylics?'

'Can you show me what you liked on the website, so I can see what appeals to you?'

He got up and brought a laptop over, accessed her website and showed her what interested him.

'The chocolate daisy paintings are acrylics, so are the delphiniums,' she explained. 'The canvases are quite large and would suit the lounge.'

'I'll have those if they're for sale.'

'They are.'

Struan agreed to buy the paintings and several floral illustrations.

He closed the laptop and set the portfolio aside, exchanging it for a large photo album. 'I looked this out for you. The garden is obviously hidden by the snow. I thought you'd like to see photographs of what it looks like in spring, summer and autumn.'

Lucy flicked through the photos. 'These are perfect. Did you take these?'

'Yes, but—'

'Could I borrow your album? It would be so handy to have photos of the flowers. I draw from real life, from memory, from my past illustrations, and from photos but only if I've taken them myself.' She eyed the numerous pictures of flowers. He'd taken them from angles that were so useful for her artwork. It showed close–ups of the leaves and details of the flowers that would help with her designs.

'Of course, Lucy. Take it and use whatever you want.'

She clasped it to her. 'Thanks, this will save me hours of work.'

He grinned at her. 'I've managed to turn the clock back after all.'

She smiled at him and her heart squeezed, wanting to give him a hug, snuggle close by the fire, to feel the warmth of being here with him.

Perhaps he'd read her thoughts, or maybe he felt as she did? As the snow fell outside the lodge and the fire glowed in the hearth, Struan pulled her close, wrapped her in his warm embrace and kissed her.

'Do you think you could ever love living in a house like this, Lucy?'

She smiled at him. 'With you, Struan, yes, I could.'

He kissed her again and she looked forward to a whole new life with him.

Sometimes their world would be crazy and chaotic with occasional pandemonium, especially when they went together to the film premieres, but spending time together here and at the chateau was what they both longed for.

They snuggled together by the fire, and he told her how much he loved her.

Lucy's editor had been right, she did fall in love with the Christmas Cake Chateau, but more than anything, she loved Struan and he loved her. And she'd turned out to be the right Lucy for him after all.

End

Now that you've read the story, you can try your hand at colouring in the illustrations.

De-ann has been writing, sewing, knitting, quilting, gardening and creating art and designs since she was a little girl. Writing, dressmaking, knitting, quilting, embroidery, gardening, baking cakes and art and design have always been part of her world.

About the Author:

De-ann Black is a bestselling author, scriptwriter and former newspaper journalist. She has over 80 books published. Romance, crime thrillers, espionage novels, action adventure. And children's books (non-fiction rocket science books and children's fiction). She became an Amazon All-Star author in 2014 and 2015.

She previously worked as a full-time newspaper journalist for several years. She had her own weekly columns in the press. This included being a motoring correspondent where she got to test drive cars every week for the press for three years.

Before being asked to work for the press, De-ann worked in magazine editorial writing everything from fashion features to social news. She was the marketing editor of a glossy magazine. She is also a professional artist and illustrator. Fabric design, dressmaking, sewing, knitting and fashion are part of her work.

Additionally, De-ann has always been interested in fitness, and was a fitness and bodybuilding champion, 100 metre runner and mountaineer. As a former N.A.B.B.A. Miss Scotland, she had a weekly fitness show on the radio that ran for over three years.

De-ann trained in Shukokai karate, boxing, kickboxing, Dayan Qigong and Jiu Jitsu. She is currently based in Scotland.

Her colouring books and embroidery design books are available in paperback. These include Floral Nature Embroidery Designs and Scottish Garden Embroidery Designs.

Also by De-ann Black (Romance, Action/Thrillers & Children's books). See her Amazon Author page or website for further details about her books, screenplays, illustrations, art and fabric designs. www.De-annBlack.com

Romance books:

Sewing, Crafts & Quilting series:
1. The Sewing Bee
2. The Sewing Shop

Quilting Bee & Tea Shop series:
1. The Quilting Bee
2. The Tea Shop by the Sea

Heather Park: Regency Romance

Snow Bells Haven series:
1. Snow Bells Christmas
2. Snow Bells Wedding

Summer Sewing Bee
Christmas Cake Chateau

Cottages, Cakes & Crafts series:
1. The Flower Hunter's Cottage
2. The Sewing Bee by the Sea
3. The Beemaster's Cottage
4. The Chocolatier's Cottage
5. The Bookshop by the Seaside

Sewing, Knitting & Baking series:
1. The Tea Shop
2. The Sewing Bee & Afternoon Tea
3. The Christmas Knitting Bee
4. Champagne Chic Lemonade Money
5. The Vintage Sewing & Knitting Bee

The Tea Shop & Tearoom series:
1. The Christmas Tea Shop & Bakery
2. The Christmas Chocolatier
3. The Chocolate Cake Shop in New York at Christmas
4. The Bakery by the Seaside
5. Shed in the City
Tea Dress Shop series:
1. The Tea Dress Shop At Christmas
2. The Fairytale Tea Dress Shop In Edinburgh
3. The Vintage Tea Dress Shop In Summer

Christmas Romance series:
1. Christmas Romance in Paris
2. Christmas Romance in Scotland

Romance, Humour, Mischief series:
1. Oops! I'm the Paparazzi
2. Oops! I'm A Hollywood Agent
3. Oops! I'm A Secret Agent
4. Oops! I'm Up To Mischief

The Bitch-Proof Suit series:
1. The Bitch-Proof Suit
2. The Bitch-Proof Romance
3. The Bitch-Proof Bride

The Cure For Love
Dublin Girl
Why Are All The Good Guys Total Monsters?
I'm Holding Out For A Vampire Boyfriend

Action/Thriller books:
Love Him Forever
Someone Worse
Electric Shadows
The Strife Of Riley
Shadows Of Murder
Cast a Dark Shadow

Children's books:
Faeriefied
Secondhand Spooks
Poison-Wynd
Wormhole Wynd
Science Fashion
School For Aliens

Colouring books:
Flower Nature
Summer Garden
Spring Garden
Autumn Garden
Sea Dream
Festive Christmas
Christmas Garden
Christmas Theme
Flower Bee
Wild Garden
Faerie Garden Spring
Flower Hunter
Stargazer Space
Bee Garden
Scottish Garden Seasons

Embroidery Design books:
Floral Nature Embroidery Designs
Scottish Garden Embroidery Designs

Printed in Great Britain
by Amazon

25484271R00066